THE SMILE OF DECEIT.

by

EILEEN R. ELGEY.

To Kathryn

With Love

from Eileen

Published in 2010 by
YouWriteOn.com
Copyright © Eileen R Elgey.

First Edition

British Library C.I.P.

A CIP catalogue for this title is available from the
British Library.

For J and B who shared a holiday
with me in this hotel and many others.

"There is a smile of love,
And there is a smile of deceit,
And there is a smile of smiles
In which these two smiles meet."

William Blake
1757-1827.

Prologue

Year 2001.
A Sunday Afternoon in March.

She glanced round the shadowy room in the hotel annexe. It was very basic. The matching curtains and bed cover attempted to relieve the gloom. Small pine chests were overshadowed by a massive wardrobe with slatted doors and round handles. She closed the bedroom door behind her and looked into the bathroom - only a white washbasin and a toilet with a black plastic lid. She wanted to ring Reception and complain but there was no telephone in the room and her mobile was lying on the back seat of the car at the other side of the hotel. Instead she made a cup of coffee and the hot liquid calmed her slightly and she began to unpack, then she turned to the wardrobe and gripped the round silver handles and pulled the doors wide open.

She screamed. Instead of a clothes rail there was a long bath with silver taps and handles. What's more, it was full to the brim with water that had obviously lost its heat. Slumped underneath the water was the body of a man. His black jeans and T-shirt lay in a heap on the corner shelf. His gold necklace glinted in the light from the lamp high up near the ceiling, and a bracelet clung to his wrist above the hand that gripped coldly on to the metal bar close to her.

'Help. Somebody help,' she yelled, but her voice echoed vainly round empty rooms. With a sudden surge of strength, she plunged her hands into the water in an effort to reach the plug, only to find that the man's feet were firmly blocking her way, jamming his leg below the tap.

In desperation, she grabbed his head and tried to pull it out of the water. His hair was cut in the short style that was so fashionable and she guessed it would be blacker than black when it was dry. Brown eyes stared back at her with sightless gaze as a single bubble escaped from his open mouth and floated gently to the surface. His hand remained firmly fixed on the silver bar and refused all her efforts to release it.

She backed away and found herself pressed against the side of the bed. She took several deep breaths and slumped down on to it, keeping her eyes riveted on the white bath with its whiter occupant. In a minute she would run for help; she would scream; she would attract attention, but first she would remain totally still and take in what was before her.

The bed was pushed against the wall under the window; across the grey stable yard was a flat marked "*Hotel Manager*." And all the time the dead man lay there and the cold bath water glinted ominously in the artificial light. With one last look at the body, she left the room and shut the door. She ran past the closed doors of the other rooms, through the main door and down the steps to the winding path that led to the hotel entrance. Young voices floated out from the kitchen as the staff prepared the evening meal. They were light-hearted and happy; ignorant of the death so close to them.

Chapter One.

Year 1997

Helen Matthews came out of her flat and walked across the old stable yard until she had full view of the front of the hotel. Saturday again. Saturdays meant coaches, and guests, and arrivals and departures. Extra staff to prepare the rooms and receptionists diplomatic enough to deal with the complaints when guests discovered there was no lift and more stairs than they'd climbed in the last ten years.

It meant organisation and long hours. Days when Andrew was engrossed in launching the latest house party holiday - this week it was to be "Visiting Stately Homes and Gardens." Although the actual planning was delegated to his staff, Andrew was too ambitious to leave anything to chance.

Helen smiled as she thought how the one thing he *had* left to chance, was her loyalty; he took it for granted that she found as much satisfaction in the work as he did. As she gazed out at the familiar scene of Lakeland hills and misty estuary she knew that if it hadn't been for Mark Wyburn she would have abandoned the whole project and returned to the noise and glamour of London life. But now that was impossible. The affair had gone too far and the news she had to tell Mark today could alter both their lives for ever.

Right on cue, Mark's familiar figure came into view striding past the gate house. His curly black hair glittered in the sunshine. She sometimes wished it was longer, so that she could run her hands through it during those precious moments when his wife was safely occupied on the other side of the hotel.

Walking didn't suit him. He needed the weight of the

9

articulated lorry to show his power. Seated high above the road, he was in command of his own world. But today the lorry would be parked up in a line of vehicles that looked identical except to their drivers who were familiar with every slight mark and difference, and would have recognised their own, even without the distinguishing number plates.

Helen turned and walked back towards the flat without acknowledging that she'd seen Mark. It had become a Saturday ritual; watching for his approach then returning to the flat, leaving the door unlatched, certain that he would follow her. If any of the staff caught sight of him, they would presume that he'd come to speak to Donna. He always made a point of seeing his wife for a few minutes and often walked her home at the end of the shift, especially now when she was so close to taking maternity leave.

Sure enough, within minutes, Helen heard the familiar click of the front door as Mark closed it and made sure that it locked behind him. She heard him cross the narrow hall with the red carpet that she'd never liked. She listened as he made his way into the living-room. She would normally have been sitting at one end of the softly cushioned couch while the log-effect fire sent flames up the chimney and her collection of Lladro figurines looked down primly on to the Adam style fireplace.

Now she stood in the kitchen, frantically toying with the coffee machine. She needed real coffee today, no substitute would do.

'Helen, where the hell are you?' his voice was fretful.

'Through here,' she called back and watched the black liquid filter slowly through to the jug below. Two small beakers without handles that she and Andrew had brought from a holiday in France, stood on the marble work top ready to receive the scalding liquid.

'What's on?' he said, appearing in the doorway. When she didn't answer immediately, he came across and put his arms

10

round her and would have kissed her, but she pulled herself away with a sudden jerk. He glowered at her, not liking the change in their ritual. He was a creature of habit, who liked to know what to expect of life.

She poured the coffee into the mugs. She'd had it all planned in her mind. She'd thought it would be easy to whisper the news to him as they lay together on the couch in the living room. But today, she stayed in the kitchen. She needed to move about and keep her hands busy, so she concentrated on the coffee.

Mark walked across to the window and stared out. 'Does he know?'

She shook her head, 'No.'

'What then, for god's sake?'

'I'm pregnant, Mark.'

He did not turn towards her, but continued to stare through the window into the yard that she had transformed into a patio with roses growing up the old brick walls. Then he said in a level voice 'That'll please him.'

'Please Andrew? Why?'

'It's what he's wanted isn't it?'

'It's not his. You know it's not his.'

'What're you saying?'

'It's your child - - - you know very well - - - .'

'Prove it.'

'Mark!'

'You're still with *him,* aren't you?' He slammed the side of his fist on to the work top, and made the mugs shudder and the scalding coffee slop over the side. When she didn't answer he said 'Well then, it's our Donna that's having my baby, what do you think it would do to her?'

'Well you haven't been thinking much about her lately, have you?' Helen shot back at him.

He came towards her again, his head jerking with anger.

'Our Donna's alright . . . '

'So you've just been making a convenience of me - - '

Suddenly he softened. 'No babe, you know I haven't.' He put his arms round her again and she laid her head on his shoulder, sensing his change of mood.

'What'm I going to do, Mark?'

'I've told you - - .'

'But it'll have black hair and Andrew and I are fair.'

'I'm not paying out for seventeen years. They make you pay now. It would finish Donna and me. I'm telling you it's not mine.'

Helen looked up at him and for the first time, saw him for what he really was; a man who'd used her for a few months. That was all and now he was waiting for his wife's baby to arrive so that he could safely return to his own lifestyle.

She struggled away from him. 'Get out,' she screamed 'Go on, get out of this flat.'

Without a backward glance Mark turned and walked away from her, through the hall and out of the front door. He didn't even bang it, as she'd expected, but closed it quietly and firmly behind him before going round to the other side of the hotel, to search for Donna.

Helen picked up the coffee mugs and one at a time, she hurled them across the kitchen. She didn't care that they smashed to pieces or that the liquid collected in dark pools that would discolour the carpet tiles. She only knew that she had to destroy something and it wasn't going to be the baby.

I heave the vacuum cleaner into the small cupboard on the first floor landing. Another week over and all the rooms prepared for the new guests. I glance out of the window to the back of the hotel, just as Mark appears from the direction of the Stable Yard. I feel uneasy, but I quickly squash it.

I rub my back and sigh. This pregnancy's different from

the first one and Mark's different too. He didn't know how nice to be when I was having Charlie. Now he's leaving me to get on with things by myself. He's always starting off with things new-fangled and excited, but he soon loses interest.

I take my old sandals off and push them into a plastic carrier bag, then stick my feet into the fashionable shoes I bought with last week's pay. The heels are lower than usual, but they still show my ankles off. At least they haven't swollen in the last few months.

I slip a cotton blazer over the red tabard that I always work in, and check that the key to the hotel's safely in my pocket to get me in on Monday morning. Then I glance at myself in a long mirror in the nearest bedroom and set off down the stairs to meet Mark.

'Been spending your money again, Donna?' he says, as he notices the new shoes.

'I've got to look good for you, haven't I?' I try to laugh it off, but realise it's going to be a difficult weekend.

'Pregnant? Call that good?'

'You wanted it.'

'Did I?' He walks ahead of me and I stand still and watch as he make his way past a coach with a London address on the side. Behind me, a car horn sounds and I move to one side as Helen Matthews drives her flashy silver car slowly down the drive. I give her a wave, but she doesn't wave back. Somebody else in a bad mood. What's getting into them all today?

Mark had better have done the shopping. I'm not doing it, that's for sure. He knows Saturday's the busiest day of the week for me. Half way down the drive, I find him sitting on the low wall that separates the new log cabins from the rest of the hotel.

I glare at him and walk on.

'Go on then - don't speak,' he says.

I put my head up, but don't look round. He can make it up this time.

13

These new shoes are catching my heel and making me limp. As soon as I'm home, I'll take them off.

'Aw come on Donna. Don't be like that.' He catches up with me and tries to pat my bump, but I turn away. 'If this one's as good as our Charlie, it'll be alright,' he says.

'And what if it isn't?'

'You keeping something back?'

'No. Just saying.'

'Well don't. It'll bring bad luck.' He puts his arm round my waist and I let it stay, thankful for the support.

'We'll leave our Charlie at my mother's for a bit longer. I fancy a lie down myself.' His brown eyes twinkle.

Helen stood quite still in the kitchen, her back pressed hard against the edge of the work top until the distinctive sound of the front door made her heart lift. Mark must have come back.

'Is that you?' She called.

'Yes, just me dear.' It was Andrew's voice. 'Who did you think it was?'

'Andrew. What are you doing here?' She dabbed at her eyes with a tissue and blew her nose hard.

'Have you got cold? I'm wondering if I'm starting one,' he said fussily. 'My head's throbbing.' Andrew had always thought of his office as a haven away from the noise of the hotel and the constant demands of the guests. He'd got into the habit of rubbing the brass plate on the door every time he walked in until the word *"Manager"* stood out more and more distinctly and the domestics knew that no matter how busy they were that must be polished every morning.

But lately the girls in the outer office had rung through to him constantly as they struggled to master the new computer system and even the Fax machine had its own peculiar sound. Today Andrew's head throbbed and he'd realised that if he

14

didn't have a migraine tablet soon he would succumb to a full-blown attack and have to spend two or three days in a darkened room with the pain swelling to a crescendo and the room spinning round him.

He'd taken the long way to the flat thinking the fresh air might clear his head but the sun was strong and he had to shade his eyes. He slackened his tie and loosened the top button of his shirt then pushed his pale hair away from his brow. He must seriously try to lose weight, instead of just dabbling with diets as he'd been doing since he married Helen five years ago.

The shade of the stable yard had come as a relief and he was thankful when he reached the flat. Just a few more steps and he would have the tablets; relax for a few minutes then return to complete the day's work.

'I came for the tablets - - -,' he said as he walked into the kitchen but he stopped short at the sight of the broken china. 'The French beakers - - what's happened?' He stooped to pick them up but giddiness made him pull back and he reached for the cupboard where the tablets were kept then made a great show of finding the right ones and swallowing them with a drink of water.

'So how did this happen?' he said. 'Funny to break them both.'

Helen stared at him and at that moment she hated his pale face and pompous attitude.

'I did it.' she growled. 'I'm sick of everything. Sick of this flat, sick of the horrible estuary and especially sick of the hotel. I hate it here. I wish we'd never come. I'm a town girl, I like life and fun. I don't want to vegetate here.'

'Pull yourself together, Helen. You're talking rubbish. We have a good life here - - -.'

Suddenly she remembered her wedding at the fashionable church in Brighton where Andrew was Treasurer and highly thought of by the Minister and congregation alike. In her mind's

15

eye she saw the expensive wedding dress she'd had and the beautiful bridesmaids and the lengthy guest list. And she remembered her father standing in the house with her for a few moments after everybody else had left for the church and how his words had surprised her.

'It's not too late to change your mind, you know,' he said and she'd stared back at him. 'I know Andrew's tall and charming but he's taking you away from everything you've ever known. It's going to be a very different life-style up there in the country. Are you sure you want that?'

And she'd put her arm through his as the wedding car pulled up at the door. 'I'm sure Dad,' she'd said. 'I'm quite sure.' And at the time she had been.

Now she rounded on Andrew and said, 'You have a good life here. I don't. I want a proper house and a husband who has some free time. I'm a Beautician, for heavens sake and I want to be back in a big store again working amongst glamorous people and selling perfumes and creams and make-up. But I can't get that now - - - .'

'You can, if that's what you really want. I didn't know.'

'No, because you're too wrapped up in yourself.'

'That's not fair. I've only - -.'

'Anyway I can't do it now,' she flung at him. 'I'm pregnant.'

'Helen that's wonderful. After all these years.' He grinned his delight.

She turned away and sighed and felt she couldn't bear it another minute. That cured your headache,' she said bitterly and he realised that she was right.

'I'll ring mother. She'll be so pleased and the staff - - .'

'You'll do no such thing. It's our secret until it shows.'

'But why - - - -?'

'Because *I* say so. I'm not on exhibition even if I *am* doing something right at last.'

He came towards her and attempted to take her in his arms but she pushed him away hard. 'No. Leave it. The damage is done now.'

With a hurt look he left the room and walked out of the flat just as Mark had done earlier. It must be a record, she thought grimly and wished with all her heart that *she* could be the one who was walking away. Instead she blew her nose hard and with new determination, bent down to clear the debris from the kitchen.

Chapter Two.

Kevin manoeuvred his way through the swing doors from the kitchen into the cheerful atmosphere of the dining room. As the most senior apprentice, he had graduated from serving the closest tables and now expertly carried his heavy tray between chattering guests and anxious young waiters serving the evening meal.

Dipping and dodging, he crossed the room and unloaded some of his dishes on to the spotless white cloth of a table set for eight guests, then he turned to table 21 and with practised ease, placed himself with his back to the sun that always glinted across the estuary and into the window at this time of day.

'Good evening Mrs Kell; Mr Kell. I hope you've enjoyed your day. Is it the nip-and-nip soup for you or the smoked mackerel?'

Mr Kell laughed. 'Can you translate that?'

'Turnip and parsnip, chefs special.'

'Sounds good. I'll risk it.'

'And you?' Kevin turned to Mrs Kell.

'The same please.' She smiled at the boy in his crisp white shirt and bow tie. 'Your mother must be proud of you - - - you're a real treasure.'

The young man's face clouded and his manner changed. 'I haven't got a mother, not a real one anyway.'

'Oh, I'm sorry. I'd never have said anything, it's just that I have a son about your age and he couldn't have managed any of this. He used to come here with us but of course he's too grown up now.'

'You're making matters worse, dear,' Mr Kell broke in. 'I'm sure Kevin understands. You weren't to know.' He took a red serviette from the wine glass in front of him, unfolded it and laid it on his knee.'

'It's OK.' Kevin said. 'No big deal. I should be used to it by now. She died when I was three.'

'How awful. Was it sudden?' Mrs Kell's face was full of sympathy.

'Yes. I found her.' There was defiance in his voice, but he placed the bowls of soup on the table without spilling a drop and turned to the next table. 'Evening ladies. Had a good day?'

Outside, a figure passed the window, just as Kevin moved round to the person sitting opposite it. He stiffened and for a split second lost his professional air. That was him. Mark Wyburn. How he hated that man.

Mark had been at the Ascot hotel a lot lately, since Donna had started working there. Sometimes he pulled his wagon up at the gate. Sometimes he walked from his cottage in the village. All that wandering round the grounds shouldn't be allowed and if Mr Matthews had any sense, he would put a stop to it. But then Mr Matthews didn't have a bad thought in his head and he couldn't imagine anybody else having them either. Kevin wasn't going to be the one to tell him how his own wife spent her afternoons, even though he'd seen Mark sneaking round to the flat in the Stable Yard. It was well hidden from most of the hotel windows but they'd forgotten about the small attic above the Grooms' Cottages, the annexe where Kevin had his own room - a privilege for a lad without any other home. Its window faced that way and when Kevin lay on his bed listening to music in the afternoon break, he saw a lot of things that went on in that flat across the yard.

He pulled himself together. Table 19 were waiting for their main course; pork cutlets in a special sauce served with vegetables in season. They were trying to catch his eye. The soup bowls were to clear. He put on his dining-room smile and went across. 'Everything alright for you, sir?' he said as he stacked the bowls with deft fingers and placed the spoons in a

19

neat pile at one side of the tray.

'Great, but all that hill-climbing's made us hungry.'

'Won't be a minute, sir.' Hill-climbing, he thought. They should try carrying trays all day and see how they felt. They'd know what it was like to be hungry then and still have to wait till everybody else had finished before they could eat.

When the last group of guests had finally left the dining room and he had cleared his tables and reset them for breakfast, Kevin was able to swallow his own meal with the rest of the staff. Somehow he didn't have much appetite left and soon made his excuses to the others and went to his room.

Reaching up to the shelf in the top of the wardrobe, he rummaged under two navy-blue sweatshirts, three crumpled t-shirts and a discarded poster of Oasis, until he found what he wanted, a scrapbook with a faded cover and dog-eared corners. He opened it with practised ease, at the very beginning. That was the only time that seemed real to him. The time when he'd had his own home, his own mother and his own life.

Some social worker with a forgotten name had done a good job of providing him with memories of that time. Strangely enough he could remember her face, and the skimpy skirts she'd worn and the heavy handbag she'd always carried, but the name eluded him. There was a photo of the terraced cottage where they'd lived, bright and cheerful with a black and white cat on the window sill, squeezed between the net curtain and the glass. The front door was standing open as if people were always welcome there.

That young man with the dark hair had come in through that door. And Kevin's mother had been carried out of it covered up and on a stretcher and she had never come back again.

There she was in the photo, smiling, looking hardly any older than Kevin was now. Not a great beauty, but that smile made her look lovely and look at way her arm went round his

20

shoulder and held him close. He must have been about three, a quiet little boy. He'd always been quiet. It had been the best way of coping with life then.

He sighed. He'd never liked the man who lived with them, mainly because his mother did. The man swaggered round the cottage in a silk dressing gown that she'd given him for Christmas. There'd always seemed some special attraction and the little boy had sensed some deeper meaning behind it all, but whenever they'd caught him listening they would shush each other and say "Little pigs have big ears." There was no photograph of the man, but his face was etched on Kevin's mind for all time. When he looked at Mark Wyburn, he knew it was the same one. Older of course, but unaltered except for the hair. It was worn short now, but curled on to his shoulders then, in the fashion of the early eighties.

Kevin gazed at the first page of the scrapbook for several minutes then flicked to the next one and on through the book with barely a pause. He knew it all by heart; pictures of other women and other houses but none that he could accept as mothers or homes. And on the last page, a photo of him arriving here at the Ascot hotel, dressed in new jeans and trainers. He remembered the shopping expedition with the current social worker, a young man this time, newly qualified and full of enthusiasm, secretly congratulating himself on finding a "live-in" job for a difficult client.

And Kevin had been happy here in his own little room working the unsociable hours of the hotel until Mark Wyburn had come and everything was spoilt again.

Kevin's mind conjured up the time when Mark had walked away and his mother had waited for him to come back and how she'd cried and cried, until one day the crying stopped and Kevin found her near the stairs. Her feet were dangling above the floor, and the cord from the silk dressing gown was wound tight round her neck.

21

I have my arms full of duvet covers and the shabby white sheets that we use for the staff beds, when all of a sudden, Kevin's door opens and he comes hurtling out and goes slap into me. The bedding slips out of my arms and lands in a heap on the green cord carpet.

'Watch it,' I say. 'What's the matter with you today?'

'Nothing. Anyway what're you doing here at this time of night?'

'Working an extra shift. We don't get time for the staff rooms when we're busy.'

'Didn't think you bothered.'

I make a face. If he'd been Charlie, I'd have given him a slap. 'Who's rattled your cage?' I say, but he glares at me and turns away. I gather up the tangled bedding and take the poorest covers into his room.

The cupboard door's swinging open and a book's fallen out. I don't mean to look, but I can't help it. It's marked "My Life Story" and it's full of photos.

He was a lovely baby; hair nearly as thick as it is today and nice strong arms and legs. And such a kind-looking Mam. Funny Kevin doesn't talk about her and she never comes to see him. Nothing as funny as families.

I flick through the pages and then I see why. There's the announcement of her death in the paper. Just "loving mother of Kevin," not "dearly beloved wife of." Then there's him with another family. They look pleased, but he doesn't. Then another and another, with Kevin getting older and bigger. Then there's one with him among eight or nine other teenagers and marked "4 lavender Lane." Must be some sort of kids' home, I suppose. Poor Kevin. What if it was our Charlie and he was like that? It doesn't bear thinking about.

Chapter Three.

In that strange Saturday lull between 10 o'clock and two, when hotel staff are at their busiest and guests are reduced to the few people who stay in the same place for more than one week, Mark walked through the gardens and slid into the timber building that housed the new swimming pool.

Crazy, he thought, to leave it unlocked. Anybody could walk in if they had enough bottle and he had that alright. He changed quickly into close fitting black trunks then walked through to the resounding grandeur of the new pool. At the deep end a single head bobbed rhythmically up and down and strong arms propelled their owner forward until with a neat twist he turned and began the long swim back.

Mark swore under his breath. If there had to be somebody here, at least it could have been a glamorous young girl not a bald-headed man concentrating on the number of lengths he could do. Mark walked along the side of the pool until the water was deep enough for him to jump in head first then he held his breath as the bright mosaic of the base got nearer and nearer and he felt that he would hit it if he didn't change direction.

As he rose to the surface again the other swimmer came swiftly towards him and suddenly Mark gasped, swallowed water and broke through to the fresh air spluttering for breath while the other man continued his way to the shallow end. Mark sat on the side of the pool and watched him finish his swim and head for the steps that only children and beginners used then turn into a sitting position and drag himself to the top where he crawled on one leg and a stump that finished just above where the knee should have been.

The contrast between the movement and speed in the water and the pitiful disability on land was a shock and with a sudden lurch Mark catapulted himself into the water again and swam the length of the pool and back with angry strokes until he estimated the other man had had time to collect himself and leave the building. Only then did he head for the changing room and the sanity of his Saturday routine.

He pushed his wet trunks and towel into a supermarket carrier and picked it up with three others full of food for the weekend, then he walked back to the path that led from the gate to the part of the hotel where Donna would be working.

I'm hot and tired by the end of the morning so I'm thankful to see Mark's waiting for me. 'Early today, Mark,' I say.

'A bit. Get a move on, can't you? This lot's heavy, y'know.'

I wish his lorry was at the door so I could climb in and be driven the short distance home. This time next week I'll be there full-time with young Charlie to cope with and everything to do myself. I push my arm through Mark's and set off across the lawn on the quickest route to the gate.

There's tables with striped umbrellas and plenty of chairs but they're all empty except for the first one near the coffee bar. A man's sitting there by himself. His short khaki trousers leave his knees open to the sunshine. One's sunburnt, the other's a sort of match but not quite. It looks like an artificial leg to me, poor chap.

'Why the hell does he have to wear shorts?' Mark mutters and I nudge him. 'Upsetting other people,' he says.

As we walk past the man brings knitting needles out of a sports bag and wool that's as green as the grass. He starts to cast on.

'My Gran used to knit a lot but I've never seen a man doing it. I wonder what he's making,' I say.

But Mark doesn't answer. He just keeps walking and I have to hurry to keep up with him.

24

Paul Hutchinson grinned to himself. He was well aware that knitting singled him out as being different, that was one reason why he did it. That and the fact that its rhythmic movement calmed him on days when he'd like to have been tramping the hills with a group of walkers, enjoying friendly conversations and exclaiming at the sudden views of the valleys or the towering mountains in the distance.

When the surgeons saved him from cancer by amputating his leg they'd changed his life for ever. He believed them when they said he'd walk normally on an artificial leg – once he was used to it he'd hardly know it was there. Instead he was conscious of it all the time. It chaffed his stump so that he needed to rub soothing ointments on to it every morning and every evening and still it hurt when he walked. Only when he was in the swimming pool could he forget his disability and feel a real man again and then he moved with all the strength and certainty of a sportsman.

That was why he came to the Ascot hotel so often, because of their excellent pool. If he chose his times carefully he had it to himself and swam length after length until he'd used up all his energy and was ready to sit in the garden and watch the guests coming and going in their bright holiday clothes. Then there was Donna, the pretty young woman who cleaned the bedrooms, a bit younger than him but just the sort of girl he'd like to have settled down with, but who would want him now? He'd never been handsome – mousy hair that had dropped out too soon and the palest eyes had made sure of that - but he hadn't been ugly either and he'd always hoped there'd be some special girl out there somewhere. But none of his girlfriends had lasted more than a few months so that he'd become used to it and even expected the pattern to continue. But if he could have had kind, caring Donna he'd have made it work. He was certain of that. But Donna had a husband and a family. How Paul envied that man. He had everything and still he wasn't satisfied.

Paul heard the way he spoke to Donna and once he'd spotted a bruise on her arm but she'd explained it away and Paul had pretended to believe her.

Chapter Four.

In May and June when days are long and evenings heady with the scent of flowering hedges, the Ascot hotel was at its busiest. Kevin preferred it that way. The cheerful attitude of the guests and the generous tips they left more than compensated for the extra work and whenever Kevin had a free day, he went into Lancaster and deposited his money in the Halifax Building Society. The pass book in its plastic cover was his most treasured possession and he never tired of looking at it and watching the figures increase as the weeks went by.

This was his passport to another world and especially to a home of his own. He dreamt of a house where nobody else had ever lived. He realised that he couldn't wait for ever to save the deposit, so in his mind's eye he saw a tiny link house on a new estate. Anywhere in the whole country would do. He wasn't tied to the Lake District. Wherever there were hotels and holiday makers, there would be work for a well-trained young man. Then he would make himself indispensable and some day might reach a position like Mr Matthews had, as manager of a whole hotel.

Now that the hotel was working almost to capacity - only room number 83 vacant, the small single one overlooking the stable-yard that was always the last to let because of the old-fashioned bath on the wall by the bed - Kevin was calculating the amount of money that would be added to his account if only he could stay wide enough awake to do his job efficiently. The problem was that Mr Hutchinson was in his usual room on the ground floor of the Grooms' cottages, immediately below Kevin's.

The man who was so quiet all day compensated for it by tuning in to Classic FM on his radio and playing it for most of the night. Why he couldn't use ear phones Kevin would never know. It amazed him that other guests didn't object. He supposed they were sorry for the man and reluctant to knock at his door in case he answered it on his knees and put them at a disadvantage. So the busiest week of the year was the one when Kevin had the least sleep. In desperation he banged on the floor but the music continued and he thought wryly that it must act as a lullaby to soothe the man. When the birds began their early chorus and sheep bleated across the hills, he wondered if he dared go down to Mr Hutchinson's room and knock until he woke him.

He made his way along the narrow corridors and poorly carpeted staircases of the staff quarters to the main body of the hotel where the carpet became thick and wide and the walls were hung with tasteful watercolours depicting the lakes in every season of the year. Low lights at awkward corners prevented him from bumping into banisters or opening wrong doors. An elderly lady in a flowered dressing gown gave a startled squeak and scuttled back into her room. Another door brought him into a warren of passage-ways and a twisting staircase down into the Grooms' Cottages.

For a moment the darkness immobilised him and he stood still until he became used to the dim glow from two lights hung high on the wall. Then he moved forward to the end of the corridor and room 82, where the sound of music left no doubt that this was where Mr Hutchinson was sleeping.

Kevin knocked, gently at first and called the man's name, but when that brought no response, his knock became louder. 'Are you there Mr Hutchinson? Open this door - - -.'

Suddenly, a giant hand grabbed the back of his neck and he was swung round hard against the wall so that the dado rail dug into his waist line and his head reverberated with the force of the attack.

'What the hell d'you think you're doing? Can a man not

28

get a bit of sleep here?'

Mark Wyburn towered above him, obliterating the doorway of the next room, number 83.

'Mark - - -'

'Mr Wyburn to you. Now get the hell out of here and don't say a word to anybody. Music I can stand - shouting I can't.'

Kevin rushed for the outside door. In room 82, the music stopped. Mark watched him go then turned back into his own room and pulled open the pine doors that concealed the biggest bath in the whole building. With a flourish he turned on both taps until water gushed and gurgled and the pipes rattled in the wall that divided the two rooms.

From the bed a sleepy voice murmured 'Come back to bed, Mark. It's not morning yet.'

'I fancy a bath. Come on in. There's room for two.' His deep laugh mingled with the splashing of the water as a bang on the wall indicated Paul Hutchinson's annoyance.

Mark should've been home hours ago. I can't sleep for worrying, so I creep downstairs. The least thing wakes our Charlie and I just want to be by myself at the moment.

That M6 is a killer. Cars shoot off the junctions. Mark's told me, it doesn't matter how good a driver you are, you can still get wiped out. I pull the front curtains back a bit and look across to the waste ground. There's a street light at the corner, but there's nothing but number 5's transit parked on it. The lorry should've been there by midnight - there's a limit to the hours they can drive these days. If he'd just broken down, he'd have rung me.

How'm I going to manage with two bairns to bring up by myself?

Chapter Five.

Paul was at a table in the most sheltered part of the garden, knitting as usual when Mr and Mrs Kell walked across the damp grass and chose a table that faced the drive. A chill wind carried the bleating of sheep from distant hills and rustled their papers as they pretended to read. Suddenly Mrs Kell crossed to where Paul was. 'Mind if I join you?' She said and sat on the chair opposite his.

Paul looked up, startled. 'What for?' he said.

'Er - - I wanted to ask about the knitting. What are you making?'

'I don't know yet.' He eased more wool from the ball with practised fingers. It was a rich brown, the colour of the soil before the fields are planted. It didn't do to discuss plans with other people, he thought. That way they always went wrong.

'I'll buy some if you're selling. It'll raise funds for the Inner Wheel.'

He gave a rueful laugh and tapped his artificial leg. 'Well at least you're not embarrassed by this, it's amazing how many people are. I was a Paramedic myself. I forget other people are still squeamish. Like the big chap in the pool last week - couldn't get out fast enough. But it served him right. He has no business in there. Lives in the village, drives a wagon. No business in here at all for that matter but Mr Matthews is no match for him. The chap's in there again now . . . I see a lot sitting here you know.'

'Thanks.' Mrs Kell got quickly to her feet. 'Thanks very much.' She turned away and hurried back across the grass.

'Oh well suit yourself. I don't know why you bothered to come over.'

He watched as she hurried back to her husband and began

to speak before she was properly within earshot. Paul heard his own name and could just make out the words 'Wyburn's in the Pool now.'

Mr Kell hurriedly put down his newspaper and stood his coffee cup on top to weight it down then he took off his reading glasses, but his wife grabbed them from him.

'Just go. You don't want to miss him again.'

Paul saw her husband cross the immaculate lawn to the stone path that led directly from the hotel to the new swimming pool. Mrs Kell had told him how that patch used to be an adventure playground with a knarled old tree that her boy used to climb - - and now he could hardly walk, let alone climb.

Paul couldn't help but wonder what that man Wyburn had to do with it.

When Mr Kell stormed into the building Paul quietly followed him. He knew Mrs Kell wasn't looking at him any longer. Mark was halfway down the pool and waved with a lazy grin. 'Just another four lengths,' he shouted and Paul knew that Mr Kell was trying to contain his anger as he watched Mark change to a laborious crawl designed to make a mockery of his long wait. Paul had seen him in the village yesterday, pretending he wanted coffee so that he could sit at one of the little tables in the post office and look out at the road and the entrance to the Ascot. Now this!

When the swim was over Paul dodged behind one of the doors while Mark changed into jeans and a sweatshirt.

'What the hell d'you think you're playing at - - -?' Mr Kell demanded.

'Ah, ah - - temper, temper.' Mark taunted. 'Remember I've still got this.' He waved a small packet of brown substance just out of Mr Kell's reach.

So that was it, Paul thought. The wretched man had even stooped low enough to deal in drugs.

'Ask nicely or Mark won't give it.'

Mr Kell glared at him and his hand turned into a tight fist, but he forced himself to say 'I'd like to buy that from you - please. My boy needs it.'

'Right but we'll say another ten quid just to make you think. Nobody messes with Mark Wyburn.'

Paul slipped away unseen. Every fibre in his body told him to ring the police. But how would that affect Donna, and her on the point of having another baby.

I just happened to look out of the landing window on my way up to check the first floor bathroom. That work-experience girl did it and you have to keep an eye on her. More bother than she's worth really, but the boss takes them on. He says it keeps "good relationships with the community", but he doesn't have to cope with them. Anyway, as I say, I was on my way up when I saw it. Mr Kell dashing across that lawn as though his pants were on fire. Straight to the pool, he went and he's not a swimmer, I know that - or his wife either. Mr Hutchinson, now - he's different. Spends half his life in the water. Bit like our Mark. It's a pity <u>he</u> couldn't use that pool. He'd be in his element.

Chapter Six.

'Don't drink like that, Charlie,' I say as he gulps his blackcurrant juice with noisy pleasure. I cuddle Lewis close and press the bottle of milk between his tiny lips. Sometimes I worry about not breast-feeding him, but I did try while I was in hospital, because I was scared of the midwife and I wanted to do the right thing. Renee fed Chloe herself and managed well enough.

'It's best for baby' the nurse said. 'Breastfed babies are healthier and more content and there's new evidence to show that they do better at school too.'

So Lewis is missing out on everything and yet he looks the picture of health. As for being content - well I even have to wake him up for his feeds, not like Charlie at that age. He'd scream most of the day and all of the night. It probably means Lewis isn't going to be very clever, but then his Dad's never been very clever either. He played truant from school most of the time.

Three years ago with Charlie, Mark was new fangled and proud to be a Dad, but I can see this baby's going to be down to me. He's got his mind on other things these days. If he's not away from home with his lorry, he's out on other business, but he keeps it all to himself.

'You want the money don't you?' he says, if I complain.

'Yes - - -'

'Well shut up then. Two lads are going to take a lot of keeping y'know'

And I do know, but I also know that I hated being alone so much. I missed the other girls at the Ascot and all the visitors with their holiday clothes and cheerful talk and apart from everything else I missed having my own money to spend because Mark counts every penny.

There's not much to do in the village either. Taking the

33

boys for walks isn't very interesting.   There's only the post office, where you can buy a few sweets and chat to Mrs Monaghan.   Otherwise it's watching the trains at the Halt or walking along the path by the estuary and when you've lived in a place for a few years, you want something more exciting than just water and great brooding hills.

I tilt the feeding bottle so that the last drops drain into Lewis's mouth then I lift him high on my shoulder and gently rub his back.   When Charlie was at this stage, he looked like me and everybody saw the likeness, but Lewis favours Mark so much that people joke about it.   I wonder if that's why the pregnancy was so awful - because the baby was nothing like me at all.

Suddenly Charlie shouts out.   His cup's crashed from the fireguard on to the hearth and blackcurrant juice is spluttering on the coal fire and staining the new sheepskin rug that I saved up to buy.   I yell at him, but by the time I've put the baby down, Charlie's run along to his grandmother's house five doors away.

I sigh and wish we could move away from Hill Edge and Mark's interfering mother, but I have nobody else to help me.   I keep a photograph of the baby in my tabard pocket and show it to anybody who asks me about him.   It's funny, Helen Matthews is really interested.   Most people only put on a good show but she drools over it.   Of course our Lewis is lovely.   Straight out of the bath and lying on the blanket that I crocheted for him.   It makes his hair look blacker and a bit curly and his legs are nice and long as well.   And his eyes - well they're all Mark.

'He's perfect.'   Helen murmurs as she hands the photo back and I feel flattered.   She isn't usually friendly like this, but they've been married a few years now and no sign of anything.   I turn back to the polishing, but I just catch sight of Helen running her hand over her own stomach.

Recently Helen had asked her mother to send photographs

34

of past generations saying that she was researching the family tree and her mother had been pleased to supply them thinking that at last Helen had found a hobby that might absorb her and take away her loneliness in that watery part of the country. So she had unearthed likenesses of people long since dead and Helen had poured over them, searching for any with hair a few shades darker than her own.

Eventually, in an Edwardian black and white family group showing regal parents surrounded by unnaturally stiff children and an unspecified kind of dog, she found what she was looking for. A boy just turning into a young man, wearing an Eton collar that pressed onto his chin, and knickerbockers - his hair was thick and black, in total contrast to the rest of the family. On the back of the photograph somebody had conveniently written the names and Helen carefully matched one of them to the boy. He was Ernest and the little girl on his mother's knee had become Helen's great-grandmother so the dark-haired boy was great-uncle Ernest and he was going to be her life-saver.

That afternoon she drove into Lancaster and left the photograph to be framed. She would hang it in a corner of the lounge where it could be referred to whenever any awkward questions needed to be answered because she felt sure that the gene for such black hair as Mark's would over-ride any other.

On the day that her first scan was due, Andrew insisted on going with her in spite of all her protestations and they arrived at the hospital with time to spare and had to wait amongst women at varying and obvious stages of pregnancy so that Helen felt inadequate to be so thin and flat. When at last their turn came and she was settled on to the bed in the starkly plain room, Andrew took the chair next to her with fatherly pride.

She looked away from him and let her eyes rest on the machine that was going to produce an image of something so far invisible. Once she had that, there would be no going back or pretending that it was only her imagination. This was real and in a few weeks time she would look just like the other women.

As the radiographer prepared her for the scan, Helen's heart was as cold as the gel that was being rubbed into her skin. She was aware of Andrew as she'd never been before - the heavy fragrance of his after-shave and the peculiar rhythm of his breathing as he watched the screen for the first glimpse of this child that was not his. She refused even to glance towards him and obstinately kept her hand away from his.

'It's coming now,' the radiographer crooned in her professional manner as a mass of lines and shapes moved across the screen in a totally incomprehensible way. 'Do you see Helen, this is your baby - - oh,' she began to laugh.

'What's the matter?' Helen said, immediately protective of the baby. Nobody would laugh at her child, no matter how odd it might be.

Andrew eased forward in his chair, determined to translate the shapes on the screen into a human being.

'There's nothing the matter,' the young woman said, 'far from it. Here's the head and the spine and the feet.' She pointed to each part as she spoke and gradually Helen was able to decipher the picture and felt a new thrill run through her. 'And here's a second head and spine, and yes they're both doing fine. Nothing to worry about at all. Congratulations, you're having twins,' she exclaimed with genuine interest.

'Praise the Lord for his goodness.' Andrew murmured.

Helen was silent and remained like that all the way home. She simply stared at the primitive picture of the two babies as Andrew talked excitely of the future.

'Will you shut up?' she said at last 'and don't you dare tell anybody. I'm not showing yet and I'm not telling.'

He glanced at her thickening waist line and knew that it would soon be obvious to the world. He could wait but then he would celebrate. One child had been wonderful. Two were a miracle. Tiny reproductions of himself to watch and nurture. He

36

walked towards the hotel with cheerful step, acknowledging the guests and hailing the staff in a way that raised several eyebrows.

Helen went into the lounge and stood in front of Ernest's photograph. 'I wish you'd had a different name,' she murmured, 'but I couldn't call a child Ernest, could I?'

As the weeks went by Helen had a great urge to confront Mark again so that he could see her changing figure and understand what his Saturday love-making had caused. She took to leaving the flat and walking down the drive on the pre-text of posting a letter, even though it would lie in the box on the post office wall until Monday morning when it was driven to the sorting office in Lancaster along with the mass of postcards showing the Ascot Hotel.

If she'd timed it right, she would meet Mark just beyond the swimming pool and before the narrow road that led up to the log cabins, a spot hidden from the hotel by mature trees. Without any outward sign of acknowledgment they would pass one another - Helen wearing some revealing garment and holding her head high: Mark whistling a jaunty tune and concentrating on the path ahead and each Saturday it was the same, neither one altering their time or their route and each taking in every detail of the other's behaviour.

Consequently, when Mark met Donna a few minutes later, he was in a strange mood and she wondered what could be wrong with him.

'Are you skiving off early?' He said one day, when she was waiting for him to arrive.

'Of course not. It must be your watch. We'll have to see about getting you a new one for Christmas.'

'A lot could happen before Christmas,' he said with a look that she couldn't place. 'Let's get going or the fucking day'll be over.'

Paul Hutchinson was sitting out again so Donna guided Mark away from him in case there was any more trouble. But

Paul had seen them coming and been prepared to speak – just a remark about the weather or some inconsequential comment that would be forgotten as soon as it was uttered. Now he felt strangely offended almost as though they'd thrown a bucket of cold water over his head but he shouldn't have been surprised. When he first had his operation people brought him hot meals and offered to do his shopping, now they waved from the other side of the road and called out an excuse to hurry on.

As he watched, Donna put her arm through Mark's but even from here Paul could tell that the man was in a bad mood. Something about the way he moved and the set of his shoulders showed his truculence and Donna looked so vulnerable that Paul wanted to run after her and protect her. But even with two legs that wouldn't have been the right thing to do. However he watched them and tried to quash his envy.

As Mark and Donna reached the gate house they saw that Mrs. Matthews was standing on the doorstep ringing the bell. The sun was shining from behind her, showing up her figure like a black and white silhouette.

There's something different about her, Donna thought. If she's not pregnant, my name's not Donna Wyburn. . . . 'You alright Mrs Matthews?' I call.

'Yes, thank you Donna. Have a nice weekend.' She ignored Mark completely.

When they reached the road, they had to wait for a few minutes, before they could cross. Donna was glad of the rest - her feet were aching and she was surprised at just how tired she felt.

'I told Mam she could come for dinner,' Mark said and Donna burst into tears.

Chapter Seven.

'Does *your* mother know yet?' Andrew lay back against the pillows, so different now with their dark almost masculine covers and so out of character for Helen who'd always chosen pastel shades or broidery anglaise and pretty frills. Perhaps it was a sign that the babies would be boys.

'She doesn't and neither does anybody else.'

'But darling, it's - - '

'It's still nobody's business. No doubt they'll have to know before they're born and that's that.'

'I can't understand you. I want to shout it from the rooftops.

'Shut up, Andrew.' She pulled her nightdress over her head and threw it on to the bed in a gesture that made him want to reach out and pull her back beside him and in the early days they would have done just that and gloried in each other until they'd had to tear themselves apart and start the day's work. Now she seemed to have forgotten it all.

'It's time we had a decent shower cubicle' she was saying. 'Why should all the guests have them when the manager doesn't?'

'Because they're paying to come here - -.'

'God, d'you have to be so literal?'

'Don't take the Lord's name in vain dear.'

'Sod the Lord.'

'Helen - the babies.'

'And sod them as well. And you needn't start holding them over my head at every minute. There's still time for an abortion you know.'

'HELEN. They're God's gift.'

'Well, maybe I don't want his gift.'

'But your body's changing already - your waist's thicker

39

and - - .'

She ran her hands round her waist line to confirm what she'd already known, then grabbed her wrap from the chair and flung it round her shoulders to conceal her offending shape. She flounced towards the bathroom and stayed there until she heard Andrew in the kitchen and waited for the overbearing smell of frying bacon. In a minute he would call and ask if she wanted some and she would reply as she did every morning "No thank you."

Today she stayed in the bathroom until he'd gone, perched on top of the laundry basket, reading her latest novel and occasionally dabbling her hand in the bath water so that it moved just enough for Andrew to hear.

'I'll have to go dear,' he called, 'time's getting on.'

'Bye' she called back and waited to hear the front door close, then she emerged into the small hallway and breathed deeply, wallowing in the emptiness of the place.

She positioned herself in front of the long mirror, placed to bring light to the gloomiest corner. She turned her right side towards it and ran her hand tenderly over her breasts and down over her stomach, imagining the life beneath. Then she changed to the left and repeated the process with utmost care.

Not one child but two lay in there. In spite of what she'd said to Andrew, she felt a thrill of recognition. No matter who had fathered them, they belonged to her and always would.

A shadow moved across the bottom half of the mirror and she glanced quickly towards the bedroom where it was coming from. Inside, a shaft of sunlight shone through the curtains and danced across the wall, transforming the patterns into the shape of naked cherubs. Two small bodies and smiling faces floated silently round the room, sometimes together, sometimes apart. Baby limbs waved in the air.

Helen held her breath, afraid that any movement would shatter the illusion. She watched the curtains blow gently and

40

the shadows move across the ceiling and back again, until a cloud must have passed over the sun and the room darkened. She shook herself and stared at the wall. The babies had been there.

She turned to her wardrobe and began to sort through her clothes until she found the loosest fitting dress that she'd worn once, but pushed away after somebody had suggested that she could be pregnant. Now she put it on with pride. When the days were cooler, she would wear her blue denim pinafore dress with a variety of shirts and blouses, and today she would drive into Lancaster to find the tiniest garments available in case the twins arrived early. Nevertheless she still felt unsettled.

Before she'd bought all the things that two new babies would need, exhaustion overcame her and she had to find the nearest cafe and sit down. She ordered tea that came in a stainless steel pot with the string of a single tea-bag dangling limply down the side. A few weeks ago she'd have had coffee - strong and black. Now the very sight of it nauseated her.

She poured the liquid into a thick white cup and thought of her mother bringing out her best Crown Derby tea-set, whenever they had visitors. Twelve of everything except the cups and then there were only eleven. A permanent reminder of Andrew's first visit when he'd made Helen so anxious that she'd dropped one of them. Her mother had never forgiven her.

Yet suddenly Helen had a great longing for home. She wanted to go now and not return to the hotel even for the time it took to pack her case. She didn't want to explain to Andrew what she was doing. She didn't want to check the kitchen cupboards to make sure he had the basic packs of tea and coffee and she certainly didn't want to touch him.

Slowly she began to plan. She could use the cash point in the middle of town, leave the car in the station car-park and ring Andrew when she arrived at her destination.

She forced herself to drink the last of the tea and finish her sandwich. Easier to eat here than to force her way through the swaying train to the refreshment car.

The long front garden was immaculate, perfect stripes on a weed less lawn, colour co-ordinated flower beds round three sides and hanging baskets that outshone all the neighbours'. Claustrophia began to settle on Helen like a familiar blanket and she had to brace herself to walk up the path and ring the bell. A twinge of uncertainty crept in. Why didn't her father open the door as he always did?

For the first time Helen thought how impulsive she'd been and realised that she knew little of her parents' life now. Only what they cared to tell her in letters. Telephone calls were put down to extravagance and kept to a minimum and they had not yet moved into the world of computers and e-mails.

Behind her the taxi slid away. Helen turned to the side of the house and called over the double wattle fence but her voice echoed round the glass walls of the conservatory and over the York stone paths. She shivered and rubbed her arms. The cream linen jacket that had seemed right for a bright autumn morning was not sufficient for the chill evening.

A quick look confirmed what she already suspected. All the windows were tightly closed and without doubt, the burglar alarm would be ready to blast out at the first hint of an invader. Neighbours might have a key but then they weren't the people who'd lived there when she was at home. She would need to prove who she was.

She leant against the wall, and opened her bag. Somewhere there was a photograph taken with her parents just after the wedding. Suddenly, she remembered that when she'd changed her summer bag for her deep brown one, she'd been in such a hurry that she'd simply taken her make-up, her wallet and her keys on their agate ring. Now she fingered the keys - - two for her own flat, one for the front door of the hotel and one for

42

her garage. But there were five on the ring not four. With a thudding heart she stared at the extra key. It had been there so long that she'd stopped noticing it. Now she moved towards the door. Holding her breath, she slid the key into the lock. It turned and the solid door opened. Immediately the burglar alarm rang out its raucous blast. She crossed the hall and silenced it.

Everybody's talking about it. When I came in this morning to start on the lounges, three different people told me. Helen Matthews went shopping yesterday and she hasn't come back. Mr Matthews is past himself. He rang her Mam's - well naturally he'd think she'd gone there, but there was no reply. And she hasn't taken any extra things with her. Sarah saw her setting off and she only had that big brown bag with her. I suppose she could get a few bits and pieces in there, but nothing much.

So of course, everybody's wondering what's happening. But I've had my suspicions for a bit and I might be right as well.

Chapter Eight.

Helen was always at home when Andrew walked round to their flat after a long day at the hotel. If she wasn't in the living room watching television or listening to music, she was in the bathroom pampering herself with a girly night-in until the whole flat smelt like the department store where she'd worked before they were married.

But tonight something was different. The flat was silent. The bathroom door stood open. There was no sound of activity from the kitchen. Andrew hurried forward – perhaps there'd be a note telling him where she'd gone. But there was nothing and an awful thought struck him making him peep fearfully into the bedroom then sigh with relief at the sight of her clothes hanging as they always did. He told himself not to be ridiculous, there'd be some perfectly sane explanation. It was still daylight and she might have gone for a drive after her long day alone or she might have gone to the Theatre-by-the-Lake in Keswick. Had she told him and he'd forgotten?

The hotel was so busy these days that it took all of his energy. When he'd taken over as manager the business was failing and Andrew's work was to build it up, gradually increasing the profits, meeting the targets the Company set him until the Ascot was now one of the most successful hotels in their chain. Andrew was proud of what he'd achieved. And proud of his beautiful wife as well. Guests often commented on her smart clothes and her blond hair that was always cut in the most fashionable style. He considered himself a very lucky man. When she got back he'd pretend he knew about her arrangements and hadn't been worried at all.

However as time passed he became very uneasy, imagining accidents on the twisting roads or simply a burst tyre that Helen wouldn't be able to fix. Should he drive to Keswick

44

on the chance of finding her or sit here and hope she'd come? Looking out of the window was no help, all he could see was the annexe opposite. For the first time he realised how isolated Helen must feel. While the flat had been an oasis for him it must have been a prison for her. Next week he'd look round the village for a house that was suitable for a family. There were some upmarket properties there that Helen was sure to like.

In the early hours of the morning he dialled 999.

The police were courteous, promising to check for accidents but if Andrew had expected instant action he was disappointed. Helen was a grown woman, she was only a few hours late and they always waited forty-eight hours before beginning a search.

For the rest of the night Andrew lay on the couch with Helen's favourite pillow under his head so that her exotic scent was with him and he could believe that she'd walk through the front door at any minute.

A few days later an insistent ringing woke Andrew from the fitful sleep of the last few hours.

'Phone, Helen. You get it. If it's the hotel, tell them I've left the country.' He stretched out his arm across the emptiness of the double bed. 'Helen? Helen!' He leaned across further until he could snatch the receiver from its rest and hold it to his ear. 'Yes? Hello, hello. Helen, is that you? Where are you?' Behind him, the alarm clock continued its monotonous tone.

Five days and still no news. He'd exhausted all the contacts that might conceivably have helped and a few that might not. Now he was living in limbo. A strange place between normality and madness. To the guests arriving for an autumn break, he was the manager of the hotel, business-like, capable, but slightly withdrawn and not as ready as usual to

45

indulge them in friendly conversation about the beauty of the Lake District and the glorious colours of the late foliage. It was the flat that brought on the madness. In there, there was no escape from the terrible truth that Helen had gone. He couldn't believe that she'd walked away without any preparation at all. No extra clothes, no personal possessions, no note left behind to explain the situation.

Yet the police could find nothing sinister, either here at the hotel or in Lancaster, where she always did her shopping. Such busy places, milling with people and activity. But the car was now a solitary vehicle in a high rise car park, abandoned after all the others had been driven away by careful owners. Who would kidnap a respectable young housewife going about her own business? The pregnancy didn't show yet so they wouldn't realise that they were taking three people and not one.

Andrew had visions of a man coming up behind Helen and clamping his hand over her mouth as she locked the car in that shadowy place or maybe as she unlocked it, her arms full of shopping, making it impossible to defend herself. Flailing arms and legs, dark car boots, lids being banged down and then later - - -. He wouldn't allow himself to consider what would happen later, except that it would be unpleasant and desperate. Helen was no match for a maniac. That was a fact. And still the police had no lead. Why did he pay taxes if they couldn't do better than this?

As one day followed another, the atmosphere became worse until he could hardly bear to be in the flat at all. Only the thought that she might ring at a time when he was normally at home and the fact that he couldn't tolerate the inquisitive stares of the staff, made him open his own front door at all. At last he began to understand Helen's hatred of the place. She had said she was a town girl. She hated the hills and all the things that attracted him to that particular hotel.

At last he understood. But it was too late. He'd lost her

and he'd lost his sons.   He'd have named them Paul and Thomas.   Good solid biblical names and with Matthews as a surname, they couldn't go wrong.   Of course Helen may have other ideas, but when he explained his reasoning behind it, she would see the logic and agree as she'd agreed with so many other things. He had to guide her into the right decisions.

He struggled from the untidy bed and staggered across to the bathroom where the black rim of last night's water left its tell-tale mark on the bath and a wet towel lay on the floor where he'd dropped it.   The shaving water was cold.   Everything conspired against him.

At last he left the flat and put on his "professional" face. His everyday suit needed ironing and he was wearing the last of the clean shirts.

'Morning Mr Matthews.'   Mr and Mrs Kell were coming down the main staircase. 'Good to see you again. It'll be our last visit this year.'

'Ah Mrs Kell. Yes. Have a good stay. I'll see you later - - .' He disappeared rapidly into his office and closed the door.

'Well. I must say he's not his usual self and look at the state of that suit.   Not like Mrs Matthews to turn him out like that. I wonder - - .'

'Stop wondering and let's go in for breakfast. It smells good.' Mr Kell led the way along the hall, joining the throng of guests appearing now from lounges and bedrooms to converge on to the dining room with the sound of cups on saucers and the subdued voices of people not yet ready to make cheerful conversation.

They helped themselves to fruit juice and cereal and carried them to a table where a solitary person sat with his back to the room.

'Morning Mr Hutchinson.   Funny how we choose the same weeks to come isn't it?' Mrs Kell said.

Paul Hutchinson grunted a reply and continued to dissect

the bones from his kipper. He enjoyed his own company in a morning. If he'd had his choice he'd have had a table for one, but at these big house-party holidays that wasn't allowed and he had to try to fit in. The alternative was to come on an ordinary week and that could be more lonely than staying at home.

As it was he watched the other guests and imagined what it must be like to be part of a family. He thought of himself with two or three children running round him, welcoming him home from work or waiting for him to help with their homework and then afterwards there'd be the quiet time with their mother.

'We were just saying Mr Matthews isn't his usual self today - - .' Mrs Kell was speaking and Paul forced himself to concentrate on what she was saying.

'Wouldn't be, would he?' Paul said.

'Sorry?'

'Wife's left him.'

'No! When?'

'Last week. But it's his business. Nobody else's.' He laid down his knife and fork.

'Don't let us hurry you.'

'I'm finished. No reason to sit.'

Mrs Kell tried to be pleasant but he walked away. 'I don't know why I bother,' she said.

Before the meal was over, Andrew made his customary appearance to announce the arrangements for the day. The coach would take them to Aira Force and on to Ullswater where they would sail round the lake and admire the changing colours from the calm of the water.

'He doesn't look well does he?' Mrs Kell whispered to her husband but he silenced her with a frown.

'Enjoy your day.' Andrew was saying before making a dash for the door to avoid personal conversations with anybody.

When Mr and Mrs Kell reached the first floor doors were open, beds were being stripped and rooms cleaned for the next batch of arrivals. Red tabards lent a splash of colour as two young women worked their way down the sunny landing.

'Hallo Mrs Kell. You back again? It seems no time does it?'

'Donna. How's that baby? What did you have?' Mrs Kell gazed at my photograph of Lewis on his crocheted shawl. I think she must have thought about her own son, Simon and how he would never have a wife or a beautiful child like mine. I see there's tears in her eyes as she hands the photograph back and all of a sudden, I put my arm round her shoulders to try to comfort her. Then to change the subject I say, 'Funny thing about Mrs Matthews going off isn't it? Middle of last week it was and he hasn't heard a thing yet. He's putting on a good show but he's not himself. Well he couldn't be, could he?'

'Of course he couldn't. Poor man. I wonder what's made her do it.'

'They say she hasn't been happy, and she wasn't looking very well. But then it's not much of a life stuck away in that flat and it's not as if she takes much interest in the hotel either.'

'No, you don't see her around, do you?'

'Oh no. She doesn't want that. I'm not one to gossip as you know Mrs Kell, but I did wonder if she was pregnant - a different look about her, lately. Know what I mean? Ee well, this isn't getting the bedrooms done, is it? Have a nice day.' I start to hum "Lonesome Tonight" as I bustle into a small room to get on with my work.

Andrew stood at his office window and watched the coach pull away. At least he wouldn't have to speak to any of the guests before evening and his staff knew enough to be tactful and leave him his own space. Behind him the paperwork mounted and the screen saver flashed across the computer but he ignored it all and stared at the telephone as if his very insistence would encourage it to ring. His mobile phone lay obstinately silent and Helen's was switched off. He grabbed the receiver and punched in the numbers for his mother-in-law's house. He had done it so many times in the last few days that it had become automatic and he no longer expected a reply. However this time somebody picked up the receiver. There was no voice but Andrew knew that he was not imagining it. The house was no longer empty.

I rub a damp duster across the window ledge of room 83 trying to get rid of the chewing gum that's sticking to the edge of it. It makes me wonder what sort of homes these people come from.

I look across to the Matthews' flat. You can see Mrs Matthews's still away. She'd never have left the living room curtains like that and those chrysanthemums on the window sill were nearly dead when she went. Now they're just faded heads and dead leaves.

It's funny that men don't notice. Mark wouldn't, I know, and he'd never think of buying me any either. No romance in him at all, but Mr Matthews's different, always fussing round his wife, especially lately. I wouldn't want a man like that. I like a man to be a man. Mrs Matthews must be bored stiff, stuck away in that flat all day, just looking on to that boring yard and the annexe window. Surely the manager should have a better place than that to live. Our own cottage is bad enough but at least there's people passing and a bit of life about it. I know I couldn't live here, hidden away at the back like that.

When I finish in there I walk past the office and Mr Matthews knocks on the window and waves me in. He's looking brighter but I don't like to ask point blank if he's heard from his wife. Anyway, he tells me to leave what I'm doing and go and clean their flat, so it sounds as if he might have done.

Helen Matthews never lets any of the staff in there to help.

She always does it herself. She's a very private sort of person and she's careful who she invites in.

It's a weird feeling to unlock that door and go in, but once I've drawn the curtains back, I feel better and I have to admit it's a lovely room. I want to start on the carpets but I have to find the Dyson first, and the bathroom's the last place I'd have thought to look for it. Funny to have a cupboard in there and not in the kitchen. It isn't a bad flat - not much of a hall so it feels a bit cramped, but with just the two of them it's alright.

I'm soon finished, but I decide to make myself a coffee and carry it through to the lounge. After all, Mr Matthews won't know how long it takes to clean a flat.

There's some nice pictures in here, so I stand and look at those and there's a few photos as well. Both sets of parents, I suppose but the best one's in a dark corner. One of those old ones they used to do, all stiff and stern. Good looking people in their own way. I think they'll be on Mrs Matthew's side, they've got that thin-ness about them and hair like hers, except for one young boy and he's as dark as our Mark. Funny how it comes out isn't it?

After that I sit on the sofa for a bit. That's when I see it, sticking out behind the fancy teapot that's in the shape of a fireplace with a clock on the mantelpiece. You get them at the factory in Keswick. All the visitors buy them. Anyway, that's where it is. This photo - the sort they give you when you have the first scan done. Well I pick it up. Can't stop meself can I? And when I look, there's two babies, not just one. I'm used to looking at them so I know its right. There they are, two babies.

I knew there was something different about Mrs Matthews lately, but twins. She mightn't fancy that. Pity she wouldn't have talked about it, but she's above talking to the domestics.

I wonder if she'll still have them when she comes back.

Chapter Nine.

I'm leaving the flat and a voice calls out, 'What're you doing in there, Donna?'

I jump and look round the empty yard. I thought I was by myself and I'd even tried to think how Mrs Matthews would feel, living in such silence all the time. Now I can't tell where the voice's coming from.

'Up here,' it says and I look at the other buildings. There's plenty of downstairs windows but only one upstairs. I think it's funny I've never noticed that in all the time I've been at the Ascot. Now it's wide open with Kevin leaning out over the sill, a broad grin on his young face. I smile back. I've taken a special interest in that boy since I read his life-story.

'You spying on me?' I shout.

'Yes. I'm watching what goes on over there.'

For a minute I'm frightened he's seen right into the living room and watched me get the photo off the mantelpiece and look at it. But then I glance at the window again and realise he couldn't have seen in from that distance. It would have been different if the light had been on inside, but it isn't.

'Hang on. I'm coming down.' Kevin backs into the room and bangs the window down, then he waves to me and I wander round to the door and wait for him.

'So what're you doing cleaning the Boss's flat?' he says.

'It's just while Mrs Matthews is away. He wants it tidying up. Not that it's bad though. He's a tidy sort of a man.'

'I'll say. He goes mad with us if there's any mess.' He walks across to the kitchen with me and round to the cupboard where the cleaning material's kept.

'That's me for the day,' I say. 'I'll get home now and start the next shift.'

Kevin looks disappointed, so I say 'Are you coming over

with me? I could do with somebody to play soldiers with our Charlie. Gun mad he is - they say you shouldn't give them guns but he picks bits of sticks up anyway and his Dad makes it worse. Just encourages him. "Bang, bang. You're dead," they shout.

Kevin looks at his watch. 'Yea, I could give you half an hour,' he says as though he's doing the favour.

When we reach the cottage I let Kevin in then leave him while I collect the boys from their grandmother's house. I refuse a cup of tea from the old lady, but I have to listen to everything that's happened in the few hours I've been away. By the time I get back home, Kevin's had time to explore the two ground floor rooms and as the door closes, he walks through from the kitchen. I decide not to say anything. After all, it might be a long time since he's been in an ordinary home.

Still, it makes me look at the house with new eyes. Just a little porch then straight in. Not a bad size living room, but suddenly I realise how untidy it is and start to empty the ashtray left from last night, and to shake the cushions on the couch. Mark likes his comforts. He stretches out on that couch whenever he's at home, with a big cushion under his head and the remote control beside him. I tell him "You're a bad example. The boys'll be doing it next." But he doesn't listen.

I start collecting dirty beakers and when I carry them through to the kitchen, Kevin follows me. His eyes are everywhere, but I have nothing to hide. This is a proper home even if it is a mess.

Charlie dashes up the stairs. 'Come and see my duvet cover,' he shouts. 'It's Action Man.'

Kevin looks at me and I nod. They rush up together and I can hear them laughing and shooting each other and when they come down, Kevin's the sergeant major and Charlie's trying to keep in step. "Left, right. Left, right. Halt.'

From then on Kevin's never away and I feel as though as I've got three sons instead of two. Mind it's not the same when

53

Mark's about. It's as if they don't like each other - sort of wary or they could even be jealous. I don't know, but anyway Kevin keeps away when he sees the lorry parked over the road. And when Charlie asks for him, Mark gets mad and says what does he want Kevin for when he's got his Dad to play with? Poor Charlie landed a real whack when he said Kevin played soldiers better than Mark did.

Paul Hutchinson sat at a table in the corner of the reception area. For once his knitting was left in the bag at his feet and he contented himself by watching the other guests as they bought drinks . . . . groups of laughing people dressed up for dinner after another day filled with entertainment. He was thankful that nobody felt obliged to join him and force him into conversation. Usually Mr Matthews saw it as his duty to talk to lone guests, so at least some good had come out of his wife's departure.

A young man in jeans and polo shirt walked from the hall to the front door. 'Good night everybody,' he called and Paul realised that it was Kevin. He'd hardly known him in his casual clothes. He turned to the window and watched him merge into the darkness of the calm lakeland evening. Intermittent lamps made small pools of light along the twisting footpath but suddenly another shadow emerged between two of those lights. The small glow of a cigarette highlighted the movement between hand and mouth.

As Kevin passed the figure the red glow shot out sideways and the boy let out a single scream. The cigarette burnt into his flesh just below the right eye. The other figure hurried off the path and away into the blackness while the cigarette still burnt between fingers that now hung loosely at his side.

By the time Paul had forced his way passed the other guests and out to the garden, both the figures had disappeared. As he stood and stared into the darkness, something moved and almost caught the side of his face, but it was only a bat enjoying its nightly flight. Beyond the lighted window the guests continued their self-satisfied conversations and drank their cappuccino coffee.

Paul walked away, round the shadowy corner to the Grooms' cottages and let himself in.   In the room above him, Kevin plunged his face under the cold tap, as he'd seen other boys do during his years at various Children's Units. Strange that he'd never been a victim of bullying there, but he knew all about it and he also knew that you never squealed.

Next morning Paul was relieved to see that Kevin was on duty; less jaunty than usual, but nevertheless it said a lot for the boy that he'd made it.

'What's the other one look like then?' Paul said and pointed to the plaster on Kevin's right cheek as the boy waited for his order. Kevin tried to laugh, but for once he found it hard to produce an answer.

'Better without that plaster lad. Burns need air to them.' He turned back to his unopened copy of the Daily Mail and began to turn the pages. 'I'll have the full breakfast this morning. I need something to set me up,' he said.

Kevin didn't answer.

Chapter Ten.

Helen knew it was a mistake. Picking up the receiver had been an automatic response at a time when she'd allowed her mind to relax and consider the months ahead of her. Andrew's voice had been loud and clear; and querulous and uninviting. She was not ready to go back to him yet nor to settle into the flat for the darkest months of the year. In February her babies would be born, as snowdrops edged the twisting paths and the great spring-clean began in preparation for the Easter rush in the hotel. She knew that she *would* return, but for the moment, the privacy and solitude of this house were just what she needed.

Her mother's engagement calendar, that hung in the kitchen on the same nail year after year, showed that their holiday had started the day before Helen came. No doubt a postcard would be waiting at home, telling of their safe arrival in Edinburgh, where they would spend two weeks catching up on friendships and buying unsatisfactory Christmas gifts. She had felt safe in the comfortable cocoon of her childhood home. Now the phone call had unnerved her and she knew without any doubt that within a few hours, Andrew would be here, determined to reclaim his wife and family.

With a wicked smile, she realised that there was no longer any need to avoid using their joint credit card. Now she would buy clothes that were young and fashionable. Her mother's things had made her feel matronly and she wondered if that was how she would be when she had two children of her own to think of. She pushed the thought away and went to the wardrobe to look for a coat to wear over the cream suit she'd come in.

Already the summer clothes were separated to one side. Pale suits hanging in transparent covers to protect them from winter dust. Silk dresses on upholstered hangers. Helen knew now why she'd needed to escape from all this relentless order and conformity, but why had she chosen a husband who was so similar? Andrew, with his neat ways and methodical mind had seemed so caring and of course her parents had been enchanted by his involvement in the church. The fact that he was older had seemed glamorous at the time. Now she knew he was simply staid.

Quickly she selected an expensive brown suede jacket that slipped easily over the cream suit. Then she rang for a taxi, but in the short time before it arrived she made a whirlwind tour of the house to hide the few traces of her stay there. The duvet cover was pulled into pristine shape, a lipstick pushed inside a drawer. A wet towel quickly folded and placed in the middle of a pile of dry ones and the expensive soap, still damp from her morning shower was wrapped in peach coloured toilet paper and put in her bag to deposit in some distant litter bin.

She smiled with satisfaction as she looked back from the taxi. The house was so obviously empty that it was an open invitation to any burglar.

'Mr. Matthews's gone then.' I say as I pass Sarah at the front desk.

'Yes. That was his car. He said he won't be back till tomorrow, but it's funny it's not in the diary - - -. I hope it's not my fault.'

'No. It'll be him. He'll just have taken it into his head to go. He's lost without his wife about. Haven't you noticed?'

'He's been different but I expect he keeps in touch - - .'

'D'you think? Have you taken any messages for him?'

'No, but they might have gone straight through to him.'

Mr Matthews'll be on the main road by now, I think. Helen's mother lives somewhere near Brighton, so it'll be a long ride. And that'll be why he asked me to do the flat. Ready for his wife coming back. I pick up my duster and flick the shelves where the postcards and souvenirs are on display. I always

57

make a point of bringing the back ones to the front so that it looks as if they've sold a lot.

While I work, I think back to the time when I was having my first baby. Mark was so excited that he told anybody who'd listen and when Charlie was born, he wet his head for weeks. The novelty wore off by the time Lewis was expected, but Mark was still very proud.

My mind's not on my work. I'm thinking about Helen Matthews and those two babies and I'm feeling a bit sorry for Mr Matthews as well. Say what you like, he's been dead chuffed lately. Funny they never told anybody though.

Sometimes, Mark says he'd like another two, but I tell him he'd have to find another wife as well, if he wants that. I can't understand him getting all broody. It isn't like him at all.

All those years without children and now Mr and Mrs Matthews are keeping quiet about it. Still I'm not one to cause trouble, but it does seem a bit suspicious. Church people, too.

'The trouble with department stores,' Helen said to herself, 'is that they make you buy far more than you meant to.' She balanced yet another designer carrier on to the fingers of her left hand. She'd suddenly had the wonderful idea of booking into a hotel for a few days until Andrew gave up his search and headed back north again, so she'd bought a toothbrush and a lot of less essential things. In the years since they'd married, it had never seemed necessary to supply him with a key for her parents' home and he would never have the nerve to break in.

However, later that evening she rode past the house in a taxi, keeping herself well down on the back seat. To her horror she saw two police cars parked at their gate. Several uniformed officers swarmed round the front door. Andrew's BMW was in the drive and Helen could see him endeavouring to peep into the bay window.

She cursed herself for her carelessness that morning. Now

he would be convinced they were all being held hostage at gun point - - - or worse.

'Hello - something going on there.' The driver announced with relish. 'It'll be another break-in, shouldn't wonder, but it must be something big. Nowadays it's just a phone call or a letter with the number of your crime on it,' he said, underlining her own feelings. What if the police started a murder hunt; dragging lakes and checking every hotel and guest house in Brighton? How would she explain her actions then? Could she say she was simply teasing her husband? Leaving home because she was pregnant?

'This is it,' the driver said a few minutes later as he stopped at a small hotel in the best part of town.

Helen paid the fare and said to him, 'Can you come back later and take me to the station?'

Suddenly the only solution seemed to be to go back home and feign surprise at Andrew's actions. No doubt her mother would miss the expensive jacket but her memory was failing these days and she just might think she'd taken it to Edinburgh and left it in a restaurant somewhere.

Helen checked her watch then clicked her tongue in irritation. 'Why does the last train have to be at 6?'

'Where are you travelling?'

'Lancaster.'

'There's an early morning one - 4 o'clock. I often get called out for that. Business men use it. They can be up there before 10.'

Chapter Eleven.

Mark calculated the time it would take for the guests to eat breakfast, hear Mr Matthews' instructions for the day, then return to their rooms to collect their belongings. Since his unnerving encounter with Paul Hutchinson, he'd made very sure he was never in the pool with him again. He shuddered at the memory of that leg cut short above the knee. Today Mark had started his swim as the dining room became alive with activity, and at a time when he knew Donna was safely at the other side of the hotel.

He left the building refreshed and well satisfied then turned on to the drive in the direction of the village. Almost immediately a car swept towards him, making him move to one side with more speed than he cared to imagine.

'Bloody fool' he muttered, 'shouldn't be on the road.' He hurried to catch up as the car slowed round the corner into the Stable Yard.

'You could've killed me,' he shouted, pushing his head inside the driver's open window, his hand curling into a fist.

'Mark!' The voice from the back seat made him pause. His fist slackened and the driver relaxed.

'That's enough.' It was Helen Matthews and she pushed two shopping carriers towards him in an effort to keep his hands occupied. 'Help me with these bags while I pay,' she said.

'Helen - - what the hell are you doing at this time in the morning?' He still hovered uncomfortably close to the driver.

'Here, unlock that door for me.' She handed her keys out to him while she searched her purse for the right change. 'I wasn't expecting to need a taxi,' she said as she watched it disappear at last 'but some fool's moved my car from the high rise park.'

He picked up the rest of her luggage and carried it straight into the flat. 'Bedroom do?' he asked with blatant familiarity. 'The car could have been clamped,' he said, 'if you *will* disappear like that.'

She glared at him as he went on 'So it's Brighton you've been to, is it?'

'How on earth - - - -?'

'Doesn't take a genius,' he laughed and pointed to the carrier bags, emblazoned with the names of Brighton stores.

'Yes, well you keep quiet about that.'

'Empty them and I'll get rid of them for you. Didn't know I cared, did you?' he said but his eyes made a mockery of the words.

'Why should you?'

'Because you're carrying my child?'

'Children.'

'What?'

'Two.'

He threw back his head and laughed. 'Hit the jackpot, did I?'

'Get out of here.' she said grimly.

'Don't worry. I'm going.' He opened the front door, but turned back with a wicked grin. 'And if you're looking for your car, it's in the garage at the back. Your poor husband thinks you've been murdered. Glad it was his money you were spending, not mine.'

She looked for something to throw, but before she could do it, he'd gone. His loud laugh echoed behind him.

I've just come over to the kitchen with the bedroom tea things, when I see Mark walking past the open door. He's got this swagger about him that he gets when he's done something good. I can't explain it, but he's different. He sees me and he

61

speaks, but I know he's thinking about something else. He's here yet he isn't here. He manages to tell me that Mrs Matthews has come back and he seems to think it's funny that the Boss is still away looking for her.

The news goes round the hotel like wild fire and everybody relaxes, but I can only think about the two babies.

Helen knew at once that somebody had cleaned the flat. It was the little things that left their mark. The ornament in the wrong place, the cushion turned back to front. She hadn't given a thought to what she was leaving behind. Now she hated the idea of somebody invading the privacy of her bedroom. Going away in a hurry meant that everything had been laid bare, even her toothbrush in the glass near the bath was proof that her escape had not been planned.

Andrew knew she never wanted help in the flat. How could he do this? For the short time she'd been away, he could have managed. She wondered which of the cleaners he'd chosen and guessed it would be Donna, simply because he was more at ease with her than the others.

Suddenly Helen remembered the photo on the mantelpiece. 'Oh no,' she said aloud. 'It'll be all round the hotel.' She ran her hands over her body and was glad that she was wearing a loose jacket, then she walked slowly into the living room and stared at the photograph, pushed just too far behind the ornamental teapot.

* * * * *

That evening as Kevin served roast lamb and cranberry jelly to Mrs Kell, he said 'Mrs Matthews got back this morning. Arrived in a taxi just after breakfast.'

'That's wonderful.' she said and her face lit with genuine pleasure. 'Her husband must be so relieved - - -.'

'Except that he's not back himself yet.'

'You mean he doesn't know? Poor man. He must be

worried stiff.'

Kevin laughed. 'Bit of a wild goose chase as they say.'

'Does nobody know where he is? Can't they get in touch?'

'No. He doesn't believe in mobile phones.' He lowered his voice. 'She's keeping well away from the hotel though. They say she's pregnant, but keep it to yourselves; know what I mean?' He tapped the side of his nose with his finger.

'It must be the good air round here.' Mrs Kell said. 'First Donna and now Mrs Matthews. It'll be lovely to see the babies when we come back next year.' She had a misty look in her eyes. 'I expect this one'll be fair, like its mother.'

'You won't say anything will you Mrs Kell?'

'You can trust me, Kevin.'

Nevertheless, when she met Paul in the lounge later, she couldn't help but share the news with him.

'So - it's about time. Married all these years. It's not natural.' he said.

'Sometimes people have reasons for waiting - - -.'

'And sometimes other people are too nosy,' he said and limped away to pour himself coffee from the percolator on the sideboard.

'You never learn, do you?' Mr Kell said grimly.

* * * * *

Andrew's phone call was specially timed to coincide with the evening meal.

'Sarah,' he said 'I'll be away for some time - -.'

'Would you like to speak to Mrs Matthews, sir?'

'Mrs Matthews?' his voice was sharp.

'She got back this morning, but we didn't know where to contact you sir.'

'Put me through' he snapped. 'Helen, is that really you? Thank heaven you're back but where the devil have you been?

63

Have you any idea of the trouble you've caused?'

'I'm, - - -.'

'Police are out in force here, looking for you.'

'Whatever for? I only needed a few days' peace. And where's "here", just out of interest?'

'Brighton.'

'But the family's in Edinburgh.'

'I didn't know that. I imagined you'd gone there.'

'You'd better call off the man-hunt and get back home then hadn't you?' She put the receiver down before he had time to ask more questions. Tomorrow he would be home and she'd need a watertight story ready. Tonight she could wallow in the peace of her own company.

Chapter Twelve.

With the New Year House party successfully completed, the Ascot hotel was reduced to a skeleton staff and those who were left enjoyed the relaxed atmosphere before the busy time began again.

Kevin missed Donna's cheerful presence and on a particularly depressing afternoon, he put on the jacket that he'd bought for himself at Christmas and set off towards the village. The temperature usually lifted by mid morning but today it had seemed determined to keep the paths treacherous with black ice and Kevin pushed ideas of accidents and dead lorry drivers to the back of his mind. Brightly lit cottages offered enviable glimpses of family life but Donna disliked the idea of people seeing her when she couldn't see them, so her curtains were already closed.

Only a dilapidated red car stood on the waste ground opposite, so Kevin gave his usual cheery knock and walked straight inside.

Charlie rushed towards him. 'Dad's bleeding,' he shouted. 'Look.' He grabbed Kevin's hand and Kevin stared at Mark, on the couch as usual, but instead of lying back in comfort he was sitting up with his head bent forward. The white towel he held to his nose was rapidly turning bright red as Donna rushed in from the kitchen with three more, equally white ones.

'What's happened?' Kevin said. 'Shall I get Mr Hutchinson? He knows what to do.' The sight of blood had always upset him and now he felt he might faint.

'No, it's just a nose bleed. He's always had them.' Donna said.

'Look at him,' Mark mocked. His voice was thick and different. 'Girlie. Can't stand a bit of blood.' He held his hand out for another towel and dumped the first one in the plastic bucket by his side. 'Go on, get out. You're useless. You want

65

to get yourself to the blood transfusion place like I do. Bet yours is fucking ordinary. Not B negative like mine.' He clamped the towel to his nose as another gush of blood appeared. 'Haven't been there lately though, that's why this's happened.'

Kevin rushed for the door. 'See you later Charlie.' Outside, he stood with his back to the wall until he felt well enough to walk on. He'd been the same when children in the Homes had nose bleeds and he'd always hoped the others wouldn't make fun of him.

Today the sight of Mark at all, had taken him by surprise, but to be covered in blood as well had been too much for him to handle. Yet in an odd way, it had been a triumph. The man was human after all. He had a weakness, like everybody else.

For the next few weeks Kevin avoided the village, simply skirting the edge of it in order to reach the railway halt - a bleak and windy place on a January day and only to be tolerated as a means of escaping the hotel.

Even the town had little to offer. After his usual visit to the Halifax he would watch a film amongst a depressingly small audience then buy a cheeseburger and French fries to prove that he was still a teenager in spite of the luxurious lifestyle of the hotel. The rest of his free time was spent in his room listening to the CDs he'd bought in town and gazing across the yard towards the Matthews' flat. Once the gossip about their short separation had died down, Mrs Matthews had settled into a quiet life-style and the soft lights of her living room were switched on for most of the day. There had been speculation that Mr Matthews could be charged with wasting police time, but if he had been, it had never become public knowledge and he had certainly never left the hotel for long enough to return to Brighton.

Helen longed for the birth of her babies. Not only because of the discomfort they were causing her or because she was impatient to know them as real people, but because it would give her a means of escape from Andrew's constant care and consideration. As it was, she had to accept his ministrations with as good a grace as she could muster. Even driving was out of the question now that she'd grown too big to fit behind the steering wheel.

She thought of what life might have been if they'd managed a city hotel and how she would have enjoyed the bustle that went on there and the easy access to other mothers and babies. Then she acknowledged the fact that without the Ascot she would never have met Mark and without Mark, she would not have become pregnant.

There was little to see from the flat, only a glimpse of Kevin in the small room opposite. He danced to his music and when the heat became too much, he flung the window up and the sound floated across the yard. Helen envied him his lightness of body and easy movement as the babies kicked inside her.

One day towards the end of February she had a strange restlessness about her. As soon as Andrew had crossed to the office, she climbed on a stool and reached down the kitchen curtains. It wasn't long since they'd been washed but it would freshen them to do it again.

As the washing machine whirred round, she picked up her coat and walked outside. A stroll in the wintry sunshine couldn't do any harm as long as she avoided the hotel and the office window where Andrew might see her and persuade her to go back. She headed towards the Pool and the path that led to the post office. In the short time since she'd been there, aconites had given the first promise of spring to the bleak surroundings and snowdrops had flowered as she'd known they would

Snow still capped the hills but the water of the estuary was clear blue, belying its icy temperature. Helen breathed in the cold air and delighted in the space and solitude. Nevertheless, by the time she reached the gate house, she began to wonder whether she'd been wise to come so far. She would like to have phoned back to the hotel but the thought of Andrew's indignation made her think again. The post office with its little cafe tables suddenly seemed a much more attractive proposition and she forced herself to cross the road.

A low twinge that was different from the kicks she'd become so familiar with, made her catch her breath and press her hand over the offending place. From behind the counter Mrs Monaghan took in the situation at a glance. 'Is it stamps you want dear or shall I ring for Andrew to come and get you?'

'No. Don't do that. I'm alright. I'll just sit here and drink a cup of tea - I've been off coffee ever since this started.'

Helen thankfully lowered herself on to the nearest chair then gave a stifled scream as another twinge caught her unexpectedly. She'd always imagined the pain would start in her back so it couldn't be happening yet. The walk must have affected muscles that hadn't been used lately.

'Here we are dear. Have this on me. A cup of tea always helps doesn't it?' Mrs Monaghan turned to the door as it opened against the old-fashioned bell causing a metallic jangle to penetrate the whole shop. The sound was somehow comforting and Helen relaxed in the knowledge that other people were close by. She lifted the white teapot as Mrs Monaghan's shopkeeper-voice kept up a patter of friendly conversation.

'And how are you today, dear?' she was saying. 'No more of those nasty nose-bleeds? You look after yourself now.'

The tea made a waterfall from the tip of the spout to the bottom of the cup. Its pale colour mesmerised Helen and she concentrated on its beauty, so that when the pain came again it took her by surprise and her cry made the others turn. A golden stain spread across the green checked tablecloth.

'Mrs Matthews!'

'Mark - - - - ?'

'We'll have to get you home.'

68

'Take my car dear. It's parked at the back.' Mrs Monaghan handed him a key attached to a lucky horse-shoe.

'I'll manage. I've pulled a muscle, that's all.' Helen said.

'Some muscle.' Mark muttered as he disappeared through the back of the shop.

'Lucky he came in.' Mrs Monaghan said. 'He's a rough diamond, but he has a kind side to him.'

'Rough diamond,' Helen repeated and wondered if the babies would be diamonds - bright, sparkling children who would bring light into her dull life. But first she had to face the blackness of their birth.

It's a funny thing that Mark was at the post office just when Mrs Matthews needed a lift to the hospital like that. Of course, they picked her husband up on the way and he was in a real panic about it all. She had a bad time I hear, and things aren't so good now. One of the twins is in Special Care and they've had a quick christening. They've called them Abi and Camilla, so that's nice. If they'd been boys, one of them could have been Mark. He'd have liked that, I know he would.

Chapter Thirteen.

Helen cuddled Abi to her as the child suckled contentedly at her breast. She ached for Camilla who was still in hospital and having to make do with a bottle. Wherever Helen looked there was a gap. An empty cot, a space in the pushchair. Two high chairs side by side in the kitchen waiting for the babies to be strong enough to sit up and use them. But would Camilla ever reach that stage or would she use the chair too much, propped safely against its padded back while she watched her sister walk and run and jump?

Helen sighed and wondered what quirk of nature had made the egg divide into two. She tried to console herself that at least it had split completely and she hadn't had to confront the problem of Siamese twins, joined together permanently in some horrendous position or parted to produce two half bodies that retained an uncanny attraction to each other.

As it was Abi's crop of dark hair was not as noticeable as two would have been and it was still cold enough for her to wear a bonnet when Helen took her outside. Both sets of grandparents had come to inspect the babies and Andrew took the opportunity to have his service of thanksgiving for their delivery and to pray that Camilla would some day be as strong as her sister. Photographs were taken as a sad reminder of the girls' start in life. The best one of Abi was framed and pinned on the wall and the one of Ernest and his family was moved into position next to it. Camilla's had to wait. However by the time the Easter rush started in the hotel Camilla was at home and Helen's life became a constant round of feeding and care. At least, she thought, it was worthwhile and there was little time to walk through the grounds and even less to encounter Mark Wyburn.

It's going to be a busy weekend I think as the cars roll up to the front door and visitors check in at Reception. Good thing they don't know what a rush we've had to get all the rooms ready. Of course it's always the same when you get a warm spell at Easter. Everybody makes the most of it.

The Kells are here in the first floor front - they like the view of the estuary - and Mr Hutchinson sticks with 82. No outlook to speak of, but he seems to like it.

The Kells always bring chocolate eggs for the boys. They're even interested in Mark. There's not many would bother. It's as if they really cared whether he'd got time off for Easter. I know they're only being polite but still it makes a difference.

'Here he is - our favourite waiter.' Mrs Kell greeted Kevin with genuine pleasure. 'Did you get our Christmas card? It was chosen specially.'

'It was great. It had the best place on the window ledge next to Donna's.'

'Did you have a good time with plenty of parties?'

'Too many,' he smiled at the kindly face and was relieved that she misunderstood his words. There'd been entertainment every evening for the House parties they'd run at both Christmas and New Year and the staff had been kept very busy catering for them all. But the contrast of his quiet room had been almost unbearable afterwards and he'd played his music louder simply to fill the emptiness. When Mr Hutchinson banged on the ceiling below he pretended not to hear and amused himself with the thought that the man might be using his spare leg to reach up with. A lifeless toe kicking out at the noise.

'So what're you having, Mrs Kell?' he said seeing the other tables filling up and the guests waiting for attention.

'Egg mayonnaise followed by roast chicken.'

And you sir?'

71

'The same. Real Easter food.' As soon as Kevin was out of ear-shot he said. 'I thought I saw Donna on the landing, I'll go and have a word while it's quiet. See if I can find out when her husband'll be about.'

'Be careful. She won't know- - - .'

'Let's hope not. That was the beauty of meeting him in the lay-by but seeing we're here - - .'

Mrs Kell watched her husband thread his way between the tables and disappear into the hall. Always so kind, she thought, risking his reputation for the sake of Simon. In other circumstances they would have enjoyed father-and-son things together, but now this was the best they could do. As Kevin served the first course Mr Kell followed him to the table and when the boy had moved away he said, 'He'll be back tomorrow and home for the rest of the weekend.'

'That's alright then.'

'Yes. I asked after that baby of hers. Couldn't remember what it was but I don't think she noticed - - -.'

'It's a boy.'

'I was left in no doubt about that. Lewis, the wonder of the age.' He laughed. 'She's fiercely protective like a lioness with her cubs.'

'She's right to be proud. Remember what we were like.'

'I still am proud, even more now that Simon has this illness to fight.'

'If we'd known what we'd have to face - - .'

'Better we didn't. We'll cope a day at a time.'

Mrs Kell sighed thinking of Simon being cared for with so much dedication at the Cheshire Home. Compared with many of the patients there, he was lucky. He was still able to hobble about and at the moment he could feed himself but the illness would progress. She'd had to come to terms with that. Some day he would move into the Home permanently, a wrecked body but with a mind as alert as ever. Then the cannabis would have to stop and they would be free from wretches like Mr Wyburn. In the meantime the drug was helping to ease his pain and they would get it whatever the cost.

'Come on, dear. Give yourself a break.'

'I'm alright,' she smiled at him. 'Just thinking.'

'The weekend'll do you good. You're tired.'

When Kevin served their next course, she said to him 'Is Mrs Matthews at home? I've brought presents for the babies.'

'Too busy to be anywhere else,' he said. 'She's never out of that flat.'

'I wonder if she'd mind me taking them round. I want to see the children.'

'Abi and Camilla.' He made a face. 'I could have found better names than that.'

'We all have our own ideas.' She thought of the two little jackets she'd knitted with such care. Their intricate patterns had made her concentrate during the long winter evenings when she might otherwise have brooded about Simon.

'Better wait till tomorrow,' Mr Kell said. 'They'll be going to bed now.'

Next morning when she rang the bell she wondered if it would be heard above the crying of the babies. However the door was soon opened. Helen Matthews stood there with a baby in each arm, looking happier than she'd ever been before.

'Mrs Kell, isn't it?' she said, trying to hide her surprise.

'I've come at a bad time, I can see, but I have a little present - - -.'

'Come in. It's kind of you to think of us,' Helen ushered her into the living room. 'I'll make some coffee, if you'll hold Abi for a few minutes.'

Suddenly the baby was in Mrs Kell's arms and she felt the firmness of the little limbs and the life in the tiny body. Automatically she rocked her and the child gazed round with eyes already turning brown. When Helen came in with a mug of coffee in her free hand, she said 'You should be here all the time. You've got the magic touch.'

'She's an angel and so is this one. Look at their beautiful dark hair - - .'

'It's a throw-back.' Helen said quickly. 'Look at this photo,' and she pointed to great Uncle Ernest. 'Funny how it comes out, isn't it?'

'We have to take them as they come,' Mrs Kell said. 'Now can I say hello to Camilla?'

Helen expertly took Abi in one arm while she placed Camilla on Mrs Kell's knee with the other. The contrast between the babies was striking. Where Abi had been firm and strong, Camilla was floppy as a rag doll. Mrs Kell cradled her gently but her heart was full of sadness as she thought of the difficulties ahead.

Chapter Fourteen.

'I thought we might drive over to Sunderland to see Renee tomorrow.' I say.

'Damn that. I'm driving all the time. When I have a weekend off, I want to relax.'

'What about me? When you relax, I have everything to do.'

'A bit of cooking? That's nothing.'

'I'm cooking every day just like you're driving - - -.'

'Mother'll make us a dinner. She'll be glad of the company.'

Without another word, he's out of the door and his figure blots out the light as he passes the front window. A cry from upstairs means that Charlie's heard him and once he's had a few hours sleep it's hard to get him back again.

I flop into the chair by the empty fireplace. It's still cold enough to light a fire but the chimney smokes when the wind's from the west so it's better to do without one. I'd like an electric fire with imitation coals, but I'll have to wait another year or two before I can afford that.

I rest my head in my hands and think of Renee's lovely home and how warm it is. You feel it as soon as you go in and she doesn't have to go out cleaning either. I let myself think about when I worked in the hospital office. Renee was only a shop-girl then, selling clothes to working men who wanted to smarten themselves up for the weekend. I was proud of myself and dreamt about marrying one of the doctors, well all the girls did. We'd give them marks out of ten as they walked round the departments looking for patients' notes.

It was in X-Ray that I first saw Mark. He'd come from the wards, pushing an old man in a wheel-chair. Porters wore white

75

coats then so he looked as good as any of the young doctors and so strong the way he swung that chair round the awkward corners. And his hair was longer, all curly and black. I gave him ten out of ten. If I had to do it now he'd be lucky to get five.

When I said I'd marry him I expected to go on working there with all the other girls and laugh about married life and bump into Mark in different departments so it was a big shock when he said he'd got his HGV licence and found this job in the Lake District.

He said he'd done it to surprise me and so that we could have a better life-style. He promised me a new house and furniture. I look round the room now - the three-piece suite was from his mother when she bought a new one and the curtains came with it because the windows were the same size.

Light footsteps thread their way across the bedroom floor and make for the stairs. Charlie's coming down and by the time he goes back to sleep Lewis'll be waking for his feed but Mark's oblivious to it all. Renee's husband uses that word "oblivious" about some of the children he teaches and it's just right.

The window darkens again and Mark's back, bringing two bottles of wine with him. He has a knack of carrying them between the fingers of one hand. I know they'll both be empty before bedtime as well as a few cans of lager that are on the cold floor in the kitchen.

'That's sorted,' he says. 'There was a roast of brisket in the freezer - - -.'

'We'll probably get mad cow disease.'

'What is it with you? You're never satisfied. I've got you a day off cooking. What more d'you want?'

I want to get into the car. I want to be driven away from this pathetic village where nothing ever happens. I want to see Renee and little Chloe that takes after her grandmother. I want to show them how Lewis can pull himself up against the furniture and Charlie can say all the big words now. I want somebody to

76

tell me how well I'm doing. I don't want to sit in Mark's Mam's
house and feel I'm the only one who's not welcome.

But she didn't tell him. She just got up and walked
through to the back, meaning to go outside and water the tulips
to make them last a bit longer. They'd made a nice splash of
colour - yellow ones and some pink and white mixed. There
would have been wallflowers round them if Mark had
remembered to collect the plants or at least been generous
enough to pay for them. Next year maybe - - -. As she held the
watering can under the cold tap a shout came from the front
room.

'Make us a bacon sandwich, love. Watching telly's hard
work.'

'Yes, it's hard work,' Charlie repeated the words like a
little parrot and Donna knew they'd be stretched out together on
the long couch expecting to be waited on. She turned the tap full
on until the water gushed out with noisy force and flowed over
the green plastic, splashing and gurgling into the shabby sink.
She refused to listen to what they were saying. She wouldn't
start to cook *again. She'd* worked hard all day. *She* wanted time
off. She wanted somebody to look after *her.*

The Bank holiday was as bad as Donna expected it to be.
Just before twelve, they'd all gone to the other house where the
smell of cooking met them at the front door. The table was set
with the cloth that she kept for visitors. It had a bright yellow
border round the edge and a dark stain in the middle that was
always covered with the cruet set.

'Sit yourselves down,' Mark's Mam called through
without showing her face. 'I'm just carving the meat. You
could give me a hand to carry things through, Donna.'

Typical, Donna thought. Mark would be waited on, while
she'd do as much as she would have done at home. She let her

mind turn to Renee. She'd have gone to the park with a picnic and plenty of paste eggs dyed with onion skins. When they cracked the shells, the eggs would still be white inside; they'd dip them in salt and eat them with thick slices of wholemeal bread, washed down with real coffee that they'd take in a stainless steel flask.

'Come on, girl. Buck up or these Yorkshire puddings'll be cold.'

'Thanks for doing the dinner Mam,' Mark called. 'It gives Donna a break.'

Chapter Fifteen.

The door of room 83 always shut with a bang, taking occupants by surprise until they learnt that it had to be handled carefully and controlled rather than simply being allowed to close by itself. When it banged at a quarter to six in the morning Paul knew that the noises he'd heard in the night - the bath water rattling in the pipes and the suppressed laughter - had not been the figments of his imagination. The room that was officially unoccupied had been used by Mark Wyburn *again*. Only Mark would be blatant enough to commandeer it, use it for his own pleasure and leave in such an arrogant manner.

Paul realised that now that he was awake, it was futile to lie tossing and turning until he became depressed before the day had even started so he eased himself up and balanced his weight expertly on his good leg then hopped the short distance to the shelf that housed the tea-making things. From long habit he'd filled the kettle the night before so that there was nothing to do but press the red button and wait. If he gripped the shelf with one hand he could just reach the curtains with the other and flick them far enough back to reveal a perfect April morning. The small garden on this side of the hotel never ceased to please him and he had no wish to change to a room with a magnificent view of the hills.

As the water bubbled in the kettle Paul balanced himself carefully and brewed his first drink of the day. A noise above him made him glance at the ceiling. Kevin was already on the move. As the footsteps crossed the room he imagined the boy moving swiftly from bed to washbasin and back again. For a moment he allowed himself to remember the days when *he* could still move like that. The early starts and the long shifts, the responsibility of being the first at the scene of an accident or rushing a seriously-ill patient to hospital. If he wasn't careful he would become maudlin and that would never do.

He swallowed the hot tea, hopped across to the bed and purposefully strapped on the leg that would make him into a whole man again. Now he could face the world and be accepted by it and he could hide the terrible resentment that raged inside him.

Suddenly he needed fresh air and wide open spaces. Above him Kevin's door banged and Paul knew the room would be empty until mid afternoon. The guests in the annexe had not yet begun to move. The silence was oppressive. He might be the only person left in the world. His breathing became shallower and rapid. He knew that if he didn't act quickly he would be overcome by a massive panic attack. The first time it had happened the pain in his chest had seemed so real that he thought he was dying yet the doctor had scorned him and prescribed counselling sessions instead of medication. And they'd helped enough for him to recognise the attacks for what they were but they had not altered the problems that living without a leg had caused him.

Now he grabbed his jacket from its peg and left as quietly as he could manage. The main door was unlocked and he rushed through it and gulped at the soft spring air outside, opening his mouth and taking in huge lung-fulls while his shoulders heaved and the pain in his chest slowly lessened. If he had been aware of his surroundings he would have seen Helen come to the window of her flat. She had Camilla in her arms as she'd had for most of the night. Now as she glanced outside for the first sign that the hotel was waking to another day, she saw a figure at the top of the steps, clutching tightly to the hand rail and appearing to be in some distress.

She turned to lay the baby on a chair and when she looked back the man was walking away with the unmistakable step of Paul Hutchinson. Helen watched until he turned the corner and disappeared from sight, apparently in full control again but she

80

wondered what had happened to make him hold so tightly to that rail. He was well used to manoeuvring awkward steps.

She turned back to the room and found that Camilla had, at last gone to sleep dumped unceremoniously at the end of the couch. Helen sighed with relief, placed one of her mother's crocheted blankets over the child and crept out, closing the door behind her. If she was lucky she might get a shower and a cup of coffee before Abi demanded the next feed. As a precaution she peeped into the bedroom where Andrew was beginning to move.

'Have you been out of bed much?' he mumbled.

'Never been in it,' she said. 'But I'm grabbing a shower now. Don't make a sound and don't go into the living room - -.'

'But I need - -.'

'Whatever it is, you'll have to wait.'

'But - - -.'

'No. If you wake them, you can have them for the day and I'll come back to bed.' With that she grabbed her clothes and fled to the privacy of the bathroom.

Andrew lay in bed and tried to recall those days when he'd woken to peace and serenity and his mornings had been a calm preparation for the workload ahead. All the years he'd longed for a family, he'd never envisaged having two children at once or the gruelling routine of their care. Perhaps if Camilla had been stronger life would have been easier but he realised with awful certainty that her problems would not go away. Never for a moment did he regret having her. If it was God's will, Andrew would accept it. As he crossed to the kitchen a lusty cry declared that Abi was fit and well and waiting for attention. In the bathroom Helen turned the shower to full blast and refused to listen to the crying child.

Outside Paul had made his way to the front door of the hotel but found that it was still locked. He crossed to the nearest picnic table and drummed his fingers on the wooden slats. He was used to his own company but he wanted people near him so

81

that he could catch snatches of their conversation and be aware of their actions.

At this time in the morning there was nobody. The domestics must be working somewhere but they were not in view and there was no way he could get a newspaper unless he went all the way to the post office for it.

In spite of the pleasant surroundings and the early morning sun the drive seemed to stretch on for ever and Paul had to stop several times before he reached the main road so that when the little shop was finally in view he had to make a determined effort to walk across to it. At the same moment a lorry swept round the bend, hooting its horn loudly and waiting till the very last moment to swerve and avoid him. For one terrible instant Paul thought he was going to die. He imagined himself lying on the road, an ambulance screeching to a stop, its blue light flashing, its siren shattering the peace of the quiet village. He stared towards the cab and saw that the driver was Mark. His face was creased in smiles and Paul knew that it had been a deliberate act. Mark gave one more blast of the horn and sped away, his massive wheels encompassing the solid white lines in the middle of the road until he turned the corner with a screech of brakes and vanished into the distance.

Paul staggered into the shop and ordered a coffee and a Daily Mail. It was some time before he was ready to take the long walk back.

I'm half way home when I see Mr Hutchinson. It seems funny. He's usually first in for breakfast and it's nearly over now and Mr Matthews is on his way in to give them their plans for the day. He's looking different these days, but then those two babies'll be hard work. He'll not be number one any more.

'Morning Mr Hutchinson,' I say as we pass each other. 'Lovely weather for a walk - - - are you alright? Shall I walk to the door with you?'

82

'I'll manage.' He goes on but I can see he's forcing himself and he's heading for his own room not the main hotel. I pretend to pick something off the path and walk back towards the litter bin just so I can keep an eye on him till he gets right in. He looks as though he's had a shock but then he might just have walked too far.

I watch him in, then turn for home. As I pass the post office Mrs Monaghan comes out to check the adverts on her window.

'Morning Donna,' she says. 'I see your Mark's off on his travels again.' She gives me a funny look. 'You should tell him to be more careful how he comes round that corner. Nearly killed one of your guests, he did. That man with the lame leg - - - sat here for ages, getting his nerve up to walk back again.'

Chapter Sixteen.

Cardboard boats bobbed crazily as their mobile moved in the draught from an open window. On the walls childish paintings depicted summer beaches where rosy cheeked children held buckets and spades and made perfect sandcastles. In bitter contrast young patients fretted and fumed in the Outpatients' Department where Helen sat on a low chair preparing Camilla for the coming examination.

She wondered if Abi was missing them. She'd taken it for granted that Andrew would look after her in the quiet part of the afternoon, so it had come as a shock to find that he'd arranged for Donna to have her instead.

Helen's first inclination had been to bundle both the babies into the car and drive away but with Donna smiling at her and Abi responding with low chuckles and twinkling eyes it was hard to produce a convincing reason, other than the true one that Donna's husband was Abi's father and her sons were Abi's half-brothers. And that was unthinkable.

At least Donna hadn't brought Lewis with her. The thought of him taking Camilla's place in the pushchair was more than she could bear - - - .

'Mrs Matthews, bring Camilla through,' a nurse said, appearing from a door at the side. 'We'll check her weight and height before she sees doctor.'

Helen swayed slightly as she got to her feet and the nurse put out a hand to steady her. 'Too hot for you today, is it?'

Helen shook her head. 'Somebody just walked over my grave,' she said.

The nurse took Camilla into her own arms and Helen followed obediently into the small room where cheerful posters disguised the importance its work. The nurse smiled at the child and said 'I guess you take after your daddy with that lovely black hair.'

'It's a throw-back to an uncle on my side of the family.'

'So is your husband fair, then?'

'Same as me.'

Helen wondered if she imagined the criticism in the stiffness of the nurse's back or if she was merely super sensitive. 'It's a good thing there's two of them.' she said. 'She'll never be the odd one out.' As she put a dry nappy on to the child she hoped that there would be some miracle cure for the muscles that refused to strengthen the tiny legs. Then she wrapped her in a soft white shawl and returned to the waiting area until the doctor was ready to see them. Afterwards, the only words she could remember were "therapists, callipers and special schools."

She drove home through a veil of tears. When she turned into the imposing drive she needed all her concentration to avoid the family parties that milled about the grounds. It wouldn't help if another child was injured for life. And it would certainly harm the reputation of the hotel.

As she approached the flat, she drew in her breath. Donna was unlocking *her* front door and going inside. Helen didn't like that.

I know Mrs Matthews had just been to the hospital and that's not nice for anybody, but she needn't have snapped at me like she did. I didn't want to work an extra shift. I was only doing it to help them. It wouldn't have been so bad if I could have had Abi at home with the boys, but no - - they wouldn't have that would they? Mark'll be tired of them by now but he's probably taken them to his Mam's. Anyway she didn't even tell me what the doctor said. Just "thank you Donna" and the door held open. Felt a right fool, I did. And Abi's a lovely little thing. She could have been friends with our Lewis. Having a disabled

85

sister isn't going to be easy for her. But then I'm only a cleaner, not good enough for the likes of Mrs Matthews.

Chapter Seventeen.

'I'm off, Donna,' Mark says. 'You know this is the long trip, don't you?'

'Yes.' I curl into the duvet, comfortable as a kitten in a basket. 'Drive carefully.'

'Give me a kiss before I go.'

'When you come back.'

'No, now.' He tries to pull the duvet away, but I hang on to it.

'Tomorrow, love. I'll be waiting when you get back.'

'You'd better be.'

I hear his footsteps stamping down the stairs and the front door bangs hard enough to wake the whole row. But the boys sleep on. I sit up in bed, but I don't pull the curtains open. It's enough to hear the engine roar into an angry start and know I'll have peace for two full days.

Mark drove furiously through the village. He passed the Halt just before the gates transformed the level crossing into a railway line. He swung round corners and ignored the speed limit on the empty road that stretched ahead to the steepest hill in the district. As he reached it he put his foot on the throttle and roared straight up the centre, ignoring the double white lines that were meant to warn drivers of the narrowness of the road and the danger of the approaching bend. From a hidden gateway a police car lurched out behind him. Its blue light flashed. Its siren screeched.

'Fucking hell,' Mark shouted in the empty cab and banged both his fists on to the steering wheel. 'It'll be more points on my licence and a fine on top as if we haven't enough expense.' He remembered the uncomfortable interview he'd had last time he'd been done for speeding. The Transport Manager had left him in no doubt as to his opinion of drivers who broke the law. Now he'd be facing him again. And it was all down to Donna - letting him come out in a mood like that. He rounded the awkward bend and pulled into a lay-by as the police car stopped ahead of him.

'Just get down from your cab, sir.' The constable was no older than Kevin at the hotel but Mark did as he was told. Better to keep them sweet. It always helped in the end.

'Blow into the bag please.'

'What? It's five o'clock in the morning - - - .'

'One continuous blow, please sir.'

Mark glared at him, trying to remember exactly what time he'd emptied the last can of beer before switching the television off and hauling himself up the stairs last night. He'd slept well though - not been out of bed once. He took the mouthpiece between his lips and blew until he felt his lungs were ready to burst.

The policeman checked the dial. 'I have to tell you the result is positive. Lock up your vehicle and get into the car please.'

'Lock up my vehicle? It's a fucking full load - - - .'

'You can't drive till we've done a second check.'

'I can't leave it here. More than my job's worth.'

'You won't have a job if this is confirmed.' An older officer emerged from the car. 'Hand your keys over. We'll do it. You can let the boss know when you get to the station.'

The phone call was difficult. Mark stressed that nothing was confirmed yet but the Transport Manager had met this situation before - - - and dealt with it. The fact that he would have to take a driver out to collect the vehicle didn't help either.

'Right, Mr Wyburn,' the custody officer said. 'We're going to repeat the test on a more accurate machine. The lower of the two readings will be the one that counts.'

Suddenly Mark began to cough. 'Had a bad dose of flu,' he said, 'it hits me now and again.' He forced the cough until his face turned purple. 'Sorry, I'll never manage it.'

'Better have a urine test instead, then.'

'Just did one before I set off. It'll be dinner time before I can go again.'

'That's alright. There's always a blood test.' A note of sarcasm was breaking in. 'Of course it means bringing a doctor. You'll just wait in here - - . It might be some time.'

When the cell door banged the noise echoed round the whole block. Mark shuddered and cursed his stupidity. The breath test would have been quick - - and he hated needles. On the other hand, the longer he waited the lower the alcohol level would be. He sat down, rested his head against the cold tiles on the wall and hoped he would be there for some time.

Driving had always been his life. He'd passed his first test just before he'd lived with that plain girl who had the little boy and the cat. When he left her she'd killed herself. It was a terrible thing to happen and people said it was his fault but he couldn't stay on when the affair was over, could he? At the time he was doing deliveries - flowers, pizzas, any work he could get. After that it had been furniture removals but there was too much lifting and not enough driving. Then there'd been the taxi business, but that hadn't paid much. People didn't seem to want taxis here. That's when he'd gone across to Durham to try his luck. He'd wanted a complete change and the hospital portering job had been it. At the time he'd thought it might lead to ambulance driving but it didn't and he'd soon realised that he'd struck a dead-end job. And the pay was peanuts.

It was only the girls that kept him there, and there were plenty of those, always waiting for a laugh and a bit of fun. But he'd soon spotted Donna bobbing about the departments. She was slightly older than the others and prettier with her black hair and ready smile. That was when he'd decided to do his HGV driving to make more money and so that he could settle down with her. And had she been grateful? She hadn't. The fuss she'd made at having to move to the Lake District had been unbelievable. And now this.

A heavy key turned in the lock and the officer came into the cell, followed by another man. 'You're lucky. It hasn't been long.' he said.

Mark stared at the window high in the wall while the needle went into the vein. He could have been miles down the road by now if Donna hadn't made him leave in a temper, or if the police car had chosen a different gateway to hide in.

'How do I get back to my wagon?'

'The walk'll clear your head but don't drive for a few hours yet. Once your case comes up you'll be off the road for a year at least. Depends on the blood test.'

Mark slammed his way out of the station into the bright light of the summer day. He was done for. How would he tell Donna that she was going to be the main bread winner? And how would he find another job in a dead end place like this?

I'm just thinking about getting up and starting some breakfast when the phone rings so that gets me out of bed. When Mark answers I can't believe it. He never rings before six at night.

'What's the matter?' I say too quickly. 'Have you had an accident?'

'Sort of.' He doesn't sound himself.

'What d'you mean "sort of"?'

'I've been done for drink driving.' Then there's a silence that's heavy with unspoken words.

I don't answer. I'm thinking about the two bottles of wine and the cans of lager he drinks before he goes to bed at night. Then I think of the rent and the gas bills and I know I'll be looking for more work and more money. But I'm still glad he

90

hasn't been killed.

> '... *Donna, are you there? Can you arrange a lift?*'
> '*What's the matter with the train?*'
> '*No cash. I was going to stop at the hole-in-the-wall.*'
> '*You fool.*'

The case had taken three months to come to Court and it had been convenient for the company to keep Mark on - it was holiday time and they needed the extra man. However when he'd finished his shift yesterday he'd handed over his keys, shaken hands with the boss and caught a bus home.

Today he'd hung about the crowded corridors of the court building until his name was called and now he was on his way home to break the news that it would be the next millennium before he could drive again. Twelve months he'd expected but eighteen was beyond reason. He'd been warned that if he'd come by car, he'd have to leave it in the car-park. He wasn't such a fool, although it was waiting for a new exhaust anyway. At least he'd be saved that expense.

He'd held his head high as he left. No good letting them all know what a blow it was to lose his licence. The sheer inconvenience of being without a car was bad enough apart from the humiliation of living in a village that fed on gossip.

Outside, he paused long enough to light a cigarette, considered the possibility of getting blind drunk, but discovered he'd lost his taste for alcohol. He had no doubt it would soon return but at this moment the very idea nauseated him. At the same time he wasn't ready to face Donna's anger yet - - or his mother's either, although she was more likely to make excuses for him and as for Charlie - how was he going to tell him that he'd lost the lorry that was the boy's pride and joy and the envy of all his friends? Even the old Escort might as well be sold now and he'd be lucky if it raised five hundred but at least it would be something in his pocket and he certainly wouldn't be paying the

91

fine with it.

As he set off towards the main shopping area he wondered if courts were built on the outskirts of towns as an extra punishment for people who had to walk everywhere. It was already past lunch time but he found an all-day cafe that served fish and chips and when his hunger was satisfied he had the courage to face the Benefits Office and arrange an income for the immediate future.

Only then was he ready to face Donna.

The train seemed the best option but as he trudged up the hill to the station a dark Mercedes drew up beside him and the passenger window slid down with the ease of automatic control.

'Afternoon, Wyburn. I wanted a word.' Mr Kell was leaning across from the driver's seat. 'If you're on your way back, jump in.'

'We don't often see you without your lorry,' Mrs Kell said as Mark fumbled with the seat belt in the back of the car and Mr Kell switched on the windscreen wipers that made such elegant arcs across the wide pane of glass and removed the rain that was beginning to fall.

'Long time since I've been a back-seat driver - - -.'

'Has it broken down?'

'Something like that.'

'To get straight to the point,' Mr Kell interrupted. 'I'll need extra supplies. We'll not be back any more this year. The boy's deteriorating and we won't leave him so often. So at least double. Can you get it?'

'I can but it'll cost. Higher risk, higher price.'

Through the driving mirror Mr Kell saw the satisfied expression on Mark's face and the car veered to the left while Mrs Kell made soothing noises and laid her hand on her husband's knee until he regained his self control. 'How much?' he said.

'Say twice the price.'

'Twice?' His voice was an octave higher than usual.
'Take it or leave it. It's no skin off my nose.'

Chapter Eighteen.

I really dreaded Mark being out of work, but in a funny way he's nicer. It'll just be a novelty of course, like holidays are, but at the moment it's lovely having him around. Of course, we miss the car a bit and we're tight for cash, but he's being really kind to me; guilty conscience, I suppose, so it won't last, but I'll make the most of it while it does.

Charlie was upset about the lorry going, but he follows Mark around like a little shadow and the queer thing is, Mark likes it. He dreaded going out at first, knowing that everybody was talking about him, but Charlie gives him a bit of confidence and people won't say so much in front of a child.

He's looking for work of course and he's strong enough so there shouldn't be much trouble finding it. It's the money though . . . just the minimum wage and that's no good for us.

Mr. Matthews might give me extra shifts, but he's already arranged the summer staff and there won't be much out of season. I've put an advert in the post office for extra cleaning jobs. At the moment we're just jogging along day to day and if it doesn't get any worse than this, we'll manage. Mark's Mam keeps bringing us a few groceries - a jar of coffee, or a packet of cornflakes, both on special offer, but it's kind of her.

I haven't said anything, but I've written to Renee to ask if there's any work in Sunderland. I know she'd like us over there and I'd go like a shot. Of course Mark wouldn't even consider the idea yet, but if no work turns up here, he might change his mind. You never know your luck, or as Mr. Matthews says "God moves in a mysterious way."

Being without wheels was a strange experience for Mark and one that numbed his feelings at first. He might have been on an alien planet that disorientated him and caused him to look at immediate surroundings as a stranger would see them. Although he was used to the open road, his days had been spent in the small confines of the lorry's cab. In comparison, the cottage was spacious. However, he was not used to the continuous contact with his family, and Donna's kindness and support took him by surprise while the children's pleasure at the amount of time he spent with them was very obvious to see.

On the first Saturday, he set off as usual to meet Donna at the end of her shift, but now the children went with him, one in the pushchair, the other hanging on to the side. As they reached the point in the driveway where the road was at its narrowest, a figure came towards them wheeling another pushchair, but this one was double size. Mark glanced at it, merely gauging whether there was space to pass or if he would have to pull into the side. As he cautiously negotiated the bend, he sensed hostility and suddenly recognised the young mother who was staring at him.

'Mrs Matthews,' he said.

'Very formal today.'

'I was checking the load, not the driver.'

'More than you'll be doing with lorries for a while.'

'Bad news travels fast.'

'Thought you had more sense.'

Mark ignored the jibe. 'You were right then - - .'

Helen frowned.

'They did have black hair. Double trouble.' He laughed and walked on, patting Charlie's curls as he went. Behind him, Helen drew in her breath and willed herself not to look back. Nevertheless, the chance meeting had unnerved her. She didn't need Mark to point out that Abi and Camilla had the same colouring as his boys.

The thought of them growing up so close to Mark appalled her, but unless she could persuade Andrew to apply for promotion at a bigger hotel, there was little she could do. Even

95

the alternative path through the grounds was banned to her because of the width of the pushchair. Given the choice, she would have had the babies sitting one behind the other, but Andrew's mother had chosen this one and it was delivered as a surprise gift.

She walked on, dreaming of leaving this misty estuary that she'd never liked. The company had hotels all over the British Isles. Anywhere at all would be preferable to this, but a city centre would be wonderful. London or Brighton or even Edinburgh. Somewhere civilised with the opportunity to visit museums and art galleries and socialise with like-minded people. Somewhere where they might have better accommodation. Somewhere where she could forget Mark Wyburn and his other black-haired children, who would always be just ahead of the girls at the village school.

On an impulse she turned the pushchair and headed back to the hotel. Sarah saw her coming and hurried forward to open the double doors. Helen smiled her thanks and said 'I've come for a brochure - the big one that shows all the hotels in the group.'

'Are you fancying a change, Mrs Matthews?'

'I am Sarah. I certainly am.'

Chapter Nineteen.

The year lived up to its reputation of dark days before Christmas and Kevin felt trapped between the work of the dining room and the emptiness of his private life.

Since Mark had been at home he had felt unable to visit Donna and the family more than an odd occasion and even then it was only when he'd spotted Mark out in the village or sneaking into the pool. Charlie was usually with him so there were no more games of soldiers in the cottage, no more sticks waved in the air while they shouted bang and pretended to drop dead. A cup of coffee and a biscuit with Donna was poor substitute although she chatted and attempted to relax in the midst of the chaos. Mark was an untidy man at the best of times and now that he had no work to go to, he filled the house both with his presence and his possessions.

Today, Kevin had watched Mark and the child head for the platform at the Halt and seen the train pull away in the direction of Lancaster. Then he'd made his way towards the cottages. With his usual sharp rap at the bat-shaped knocker, he'd opened the door and walked straight in. As usual the scene comforted him. A bright fire burned behind the high guard and Lewis toddled towards him through the clutter of scattered toys, damp clothes attempting to dry near the fireplace and empty cups standing where Mark had abandoned them.

'Anybody in?' Kevin called.

'Come through.' Donna's voice was muffled and the whirr of the washing machine competed to fill the place with noise. In the kitchen a wooden ironing board was set up and a blue plastic container overflowed with shabby garments that Donna selected, ironed and folded at an incredible speed.

Kevin leaned against a work top and watched her.

Something about her movements stirred a memory in his brain and he struggled to grasp it. He was a child again, very small, and his own mother stood in another kitchen ironing a silk dressing gown while its owner stood watching. They laughed together and joked about the brief underwear the man was wearing while he waited for her to finish. When the garment was ready the man had put it on, feeling its warmth and pulling Kevin's mother into it so that her head nestled against his chest and she felt safe and loved.

It wasn't long after that, that the man left and Kevin's life had changed for ever. Suddenly he couldn't look at Donna or stay in her kitchen. 'Just remembered something,' he muttered and rushed into the living room, skirting round Lewis as he pushed a toy car across the floor. Then he dodged through the front door and away in the direction of the estuary, to walk at the water's edge until the darkness made it unsafe to stay any longer. Only then did he return to the hotel.

It was nice to see Kevin this afternoon. It would have been a good excuse to stop for a bit and have a cup of coffee but he went shooting off. Surely he wasn't offended because I didn't stop straight away - he's nearly one of the family, now although I must say he hasn't come much since Mark was at home. But then they don't get on and Charlie's at nursery in the mornings and Lewis is too little to play yet. Oh dear there's always something to worry about.

I did run to the door and try to catch Kevin but he'd gone, and not towards the Ascot either or I'd have seen him. He's a nice lad and he must be lonely, especially with Christmas coming on and no home to go back to. He could come to us, as far as I'm concerned but Mark wouldn't like it and then there's his Mam

When the big parties start Kevin'll be too busy to think much. And hopefully I will as well. If I don't get some extra

98

money I don't know how we're going to manage. Renee's looking out for something over there and I must say Mark doesn't complain. The funny thing is he manages to make his money go round.

As Kevin took a short cut across the lawn he saw that a Christmas tree was standing in the square bay window of the main lounge. His young colleagues laughed and chattered as they hung baubles and fixed tiny white lights to every branch. If he went inside he would immediately be part of the activity, welcomed and included by them all, but while he stayed outside he could be detached and view the hotel with a different eye.

Another Christmas starting, another round of House parties and enormous meals where guests vied to be best-dressed and crackers produced gaudy hats and useless gifts that were abandoned when the meal was over.

Suddenly a taxi rounded the bend, its headlights catching him in their beam so that he moved away, reluctant to be seen as a peeping Tom outside the window. As soon as the car stopped the driver jumped out while the back door opened more slowly and the unmistakable figure of Paul Hutchinson emerged.

'Here boy,' he called. 'Give me a hand with these bags. Better than standing there like a frightened rabbit.'

'Mr Hutchinson, is that you?'

'Who else d'you know, walks like this?'

Kevin picked up the luggage and gauged that it was going to be a long stay. 'Usual room, is it?'

'82. Suits me.'

Another Christmas listening to Classic FM all night and getting up bleary-eyed for the busiest time of the year. He wouldn't do it again. By next year he'd be miles away. Somewhere where they didn't have a Paul Hutchinson. With any luck at all Kevin might be able to buy his own property - but it wouldn't be an upstairs flat. He'd make sure of that.

Chapter Twenty.

Months passed and still Andrew was managing the Ascot hotel.

One day Helen struggled to hold on to Abi while she slotted her plump little legs into black trousers. She'd already managed to ease a white jumper over the child's dark curls and make a game of the way her head popped through the polo neck, showing bright eyes, alive with joy. As a final touch Helen pinned a colourful badge on to her jumper with the message "2 Today." Patent leather shoes almost reflected Abi's smile as she bent down to admire their newness.

Then Helen turned, to repeat the process with Camilla who had been watching from the comfort of a pushchair. Soon she would need a new one - blue and white stripes and a light-weight frame singling it out as a first wheel-chair. However the excitement in Camilla's face was there just as clearly as in her sister's and if her limbs occasionally jumped with uncontrolled movement it only added to the happiness of the day. With great tenderness Helen lifted her on to her knee and dressed her in an identical outfit to Abi's chosen specially to enhance this child's appearance. When *her* badge was finally in place Camilla managed to fling one arm out with an erratic movement that brought her hand flatly across it in a way that expressed her pleasure as surely as any words could have done. Helen cuddled her and kissed the top of her head.

Two years since their birth and Andrew was as satisfied now as he had been then and although Helen lived every day in the knowledge of Mark's presence Andrew simply recognised him as the husband of one of his staff who'd put the livelihood of his whole family in jeopardy. Teetotal himself, Andrew had no patience with those who weren't. Nevertheless, he considered it his duty to do what he could to help Donna support her family so he found it hard to understand Helen's opposition to the idea of offering Donna the post of Mother's Help.

He even wondered if Helen was becoming too possessive of Camilla. He had been thankful when his parents confirmed his fears and persuaded him that the expense of extra help would benefit Abi. Helen's reaction to the trifling birthday presents he'd given them and the knowledge that a lump sum had been invested had been disappointing in the least. In fact it had resulted in the worst row they'd ever had.

'When I want help I'll ask for it. I don't need Donna or anybody else.' She had screamed at him. 'They're my children and I'll look after them any way I want to.'

'But they're my children, too - - - .'

'Huh!'

'And Abi can't be held back because of Camilla.'

'Go on, suggest we put her in an institution, why don't you? She's a disappointment, isn't she? A slur on your manhood as they used to say.'

'No, of course she isn't but she'll never reach Abi's standards.'

'You don't know that. She understands everything but she'll need help to express it. Save your money for that.'

'It would help Donna too. You know her husband's lost his job.'

'Nothing to do with us.'

He'd stormed out and she really didn't care whether he came back for the party or not. However, she knew he would if only to show himself as the perfect father. Strangely enough the girls saw him as that too. Helen found it hard to accept their delight whenever he came into the flat. If she'd had thoughts of ending the marriage this was surely a reason to prevent it, just as the threat of Donna's help was going to prevent Helen from looking for the work she'd promised herself as soon as the girls passed the baby stage.

She'd already discovered a nursery that would accept Camilla as well as Abi but the cost would be exorbitant and she knew Andrew would never agree to that. The independence she craved was relegated to her dreams.

Nevertheless when the party was over she put on a false smile and told Andrew how well he'd done and he basked in the praise as she'd known he would.

'You're wasted here,' she said. 'You could be running one of the big city hotels.'

'But we'd miss the country air.'

'Everybody has to make sacrifices and think of the opportunities for the girls.'

He'd been non-committal but he'd smiled at the idea as he returned to the office.

Nothing's come of the advert in the post office. I thought it might, but I suppose everybody's fixed up. Funny - I had a feeling Mr Matthews was going to offer me something, like helping with the twins and I'd have liked that. It would've been a change from cleaning and it might have gone on for years with Camilla being the way she is. Anyway it didn't happen. I must have imagined it, but he did start asking whether I liked looking after children. Of course I said I did and I could always have fitted Lewis in with them when Mark manages to find a job.

If we get across to Sunderland Renee'll help with the boys. I know she will. Doesn't want any more of her own but she likes minding mine - - and handing them back.

Last I heard, she was finding out about a car factory at Washington. It's not that far from Sunderland and there must be plenty of people that would give Mark a lift, if the shifts are awkward.

Chapter Twenty One.

A brown envelope was lying on the mat. It looked like a bill, so Donna left it. There was no need to get upset before she'd had her first cup of tea in the morning. She drank the tea slowly; it was weaker than she liked it. There was just one bag in the pot these days. She made a slice of toast and scraped a bit of marmalade on to it. Doing without butter was working wonders with her waist-line.

She refused to think about the envelope and whether it was from the electric people or the gas. The next thing would be the television licence. She should have had a new one before Christmas, but it had been the last thing on her mind. She'd usually bought savings stamps, when she was collecting her child-allowance, but she'd missed a few times since last September, always intending to buy double next time but she never did. And now the van was in the district. If they lost their television, Mark would be furious and Donna felt sure she was the one who would have to go to court. She'd heard that it was the person in the house at the time so it was most likely to be her. She would have to get a licence somehow, but didn't know where she was going to find money like that.

While she was thinking about it, she wandered back into the living-room. The sun was shining straight on to the envelope, so she couldn't ignore it any longer. Now she could see that the address was written in blue ink, not typed like they usually were. She hoped it was an answer to her advertisement in the post office. She'd given her address, in case the phone was cut off. When she picked the letter up she discovered it was Renee's writing; she could have been reading it all the time she was drinking her tea, but Renee had never used brown envelopes before.

Donna ripped it open, and found only a short letter, but a

103

lot of newspaper cuttings. When she laid them on the table, she realised they were job adverts for Mark. Suddenly the day seemed brighter.

The main one was for the big car factory near Sunderland. They were changing the shift patterns, so they needed more Production Workers. "Good rate of pay," it said. "Experience preferred but not essential." Donna wondered if driving counted. It wasn't the same as making cars, but it meant Mark was used to them. He knew what held the wheels on and he was a whizz with engines. And he understood about putting the seats in and the dash boards and everything. He'd been around cars all his life. You could say cars *were* his life, so he should stand a good chance.

Then there was another - "Daytime Traffic Controller with experience of routing and scheduling vehicles." He could do that. He knew the routes all over the country and Donna supposed he'd understand about scheduling, and he'd soon pick up the keyboard skills. Everybody did these days.

"Run Your Own Pub." Brilliant idea. She could be behind the bar and listen out for the boys at the same time. That would solve the problem of where to live, and she supposed it wouldn't matter about Mark losing his licence, because he wouldn't have to drive anywhere.

She picked up another cutting. "Vehicle Preparation Operative . . . must have at least five years' experience." She crumpled the paper and threw it in the bin.

The rest were for Agencies. Donna didn't know how they worked, but Mark could ring and find out.

It's all looking good. I knew I could rely on Renee. Once he's settled in, we'll move over there and rent a place, and it'll be lovely to be near her again, instead of his Mam. And in a city there'll be good schools for the boys and a job for me as well, I shouldn't wonder.

I might get back into an office. I'd better start taking care of my hands and see if I can get them the way they were in the hospital days, all smooth and nice, and I might wear nail varnish again as well. A lot's happened since then. I meant to keep in touch with everybody, but I'll make new friends when I get there. I hope Renee'll let Mark stay with them for a bit till he gets settled.

'What's all this then?' Mark had come downstairs too quietly. Donna hadn't meant him to find out like this. She'd intended to break it to him gently later in the day; choosing a time when he was in a good mood, or he'd had his first drink. He could see she was flustered now, as she tried to stammer out an explanation.

'What's going on?' he said and picked up one of the advertisements. 'Production Workers wanted,' he read out. 'And where d'you think this is? Eh where?'

'It's near our Renee. She's sent them. She's trying to help.'

'Trying to get you back there, more like. Well she can stuff her adverts *and* her production jobs. I'm an outside man, and I'm staying that way.'

He stormed into the yard, but he didn't destroy the cuttings and Donna pushed them back into the envelope as fast as she could, then hid them behind the packet of Bold. That's one thing he never touched. She would try him again later. She was not giving up yet.

Mark lit a cigarette, inhaling deeply as he stared beyond the whitewashed wall. It was a long time since he'd come out here. Yards were for women and washing lines and plants in pots, but today he needed to look at the hills, still in morning shadow, but be there for ever, just as *he* wanted to be.

On all his journeys, he'd never found anywhere he liked better than Hill Edge. He kicked at a plastic soldier that Charlie had left on the rough grey concrete, then watched it rise above a green tub and hit the old wall before it dropped on to the soil below.

Donna was a traitor. Going behind his back and plotting with that sister of hers. And if she thought he was going to live in the same house as that smarmy schoolteacher, she had another think coming. It would soon be Easter and he'd heard that the Kells were coming back so there'd be the chance to do a bit of business again. That was something else he'd missed. And another whole year to get through yet. He flung the butt of his cigarette down and ground it under his heavy boot. In the distance, traffic roared along the road and drivers changed gear as they approached a roundabout. Behind the cottage, the 7.45 train gathered speed on its way to Lancaster.

Mark turned on his heel and slammed back into the cottage. Donna's voice came from upstairs, chiding the children about something they'd either done or not done. He didn't care which. He wanted to be in his lorry and away from all this domesticity. He strode straight through the living room and out into the street. From five doors away, his mother called a cheery good morning, resting her sweeping brush against the reddened window ledge and preparing for a lengthy conversation. Mark gave her a brief acknowledgment and turned the opposite way.

He'd managed to make extra money. He had his contacts and Mr Kell would be wanting a good order to see them through the summer, but it wasn't enough, even though Donna worked wonders with their official income.

He could hardly bear to walk through the village these days. The narrow pavement was so close to the traffic, if he stretched out a hand, he could touch the cars as they passed and when a lorry trundled through, Mark inspected the wheels with expert eyes. Its canvas sides were drawn back, protection against high winds and illegal immigrants. Mark visualised how it would be loaded at some nearby depot; what it would carry and where it would go. A great ache filled him. He wanted to be up there in the cab, feeling the steering wheel in his strong hands and changing gear as he approached heavy traffic or negotiated awkward bends. He wanted to see the road ahead of him. He wanted freedom.

But all he could do was walk, faster and faster until people stared and wondered whether he was practising for the Great North Run. One or two called a greeting, but he neither eard nor cared. Trapped, that's what he was. Trapped in this village with nothing but a post office, a hotel and a railway halt. Without wheels and without money.

He crossed the road and automatically took the path into the hotel. As he approached the pool, he saw that one of the staff was unlocking the door. On an impulse, he sidled in as the man disappeared from sight. The emptiness of the place reminded him of a cathedral his mother had once dragged him into, when she'd been determined he would see everything there was to see. Secretly, its vastness had impressed him and for a short time he'd been silenced by its atmosphere. Now he stood at the head of the pool and savoured the feeling that he was the first person to be there, that morning.

Guessing that everybody would be safely at breakfast, he stripped off his clothes, left them exactly where they fell and dived in to the warm, blue water. With angry strokes and clear direction, he headed for the opposite end. As always, the exercise calmed him and by the time he'd done two lengths he felt relaxed enough to jump out and head for the changing room in search of something to use as a towel.

As he put his hand towards the door, it opened from the inside and Paul Hutchinson came through, crawling, without his artificial leg. The two men paused and stared, each shocked by the other's appearance then they hurried on without a word.

107

Chapter Twenty-Two.

On Easter Saturday Mark mingled with the group of guests that were gathering for an afternoon trip to see the daffodils. He hated the nonchalant way people carried their cameras and the trusting attitude as somebody laid an expensive one on to an outside bench while zipping up her jacket against the breeze that was deceptively cool in the spring sunshine.

He had to thrust his hands deep into his pockets to avoid temptation as he passed between the bench and the owner of the camera. She deserved to lose it, he thought, but theft was something he didn't go for. A bit of dealing was one thing - business, if you like - and it involved both parties but stealing, that was downright criminal and he'd need to be pushed to the limit for that.

He scanned the crowd, knowing that he would easily recognise the Kells amongst the first-time guests but as the coach arrived and negotiated a difficult three-point turn they still did not appear. 'Fuck it!' He said under his breath. It had been the same yesterday. The garden full of people enjoying the first day of the holiday, but no sign of Mr and Mrs Kell.

Now he flung the hotel door open and pushed his way towards Sarah who was giving instructions to somebody about the dangers of hill-walking.

'Donna ready yet?' he called.

'Kitchen door,' she said and glared at him.

His face darkened but he left without a word, just in time to see the coach pull away. Framed in its back window were the unmistakable figures of the Kells. He had the distinct feeling that Mrs Kell was going to acknowledge him, but a movement from her husband stopped her. Mark fingered the expensive drugs in his pocket, then he strode away to the kitchen to wait for Donna.

108

As he turned towards the Grooms' Cottages Abi came running unsteadily from the stable yard and almost collided with him so that when Helen hurried after her she was met by the sight of the little girl holding Mark's hand and staring up into his face.

'Abi, what're you doing?' she shouted and quickly scooped the child into her arms.

'Running away by the looks of it.' Mark said. 'You want to be more careful. She's special.'

Without a word Helen turned and hurried back to the flat where she banged the door shut and put the chain in place. As soon as she was in the living room she picked up the phone and rang the hotel's head office. 'Hello, I'm speaking for Mr Matthews, manager of the Ascot hotel,' she said when the answer phone announced that the office was closed until Tuesday and invited her to leave a message. 'He'd like some information about vacancies in any of the city hotels - - - , as soon as possible please. Thank you. Goodbye.'

Behind her Camilla let out an anguished cry and Abi giggled excitedly.

Mark doesn't like coming to the kitchen door. He has this thing about us being as good as anybody else, but Mr Matthews won't have staff mixing with guests and there's an excursion leaving from the front. I see Mr and Mrs Kell are down for it but I could swear they're dodging me and she hasn't given me the chocolate eggs for the boys so far. Still, there's plenty of the weekend left yet, so we'll see what happens.

Anyway, when Mark arrives he's looking pleased with himself. I hate that look. It means something's happened that he's not telling me. I feel all left out and awkward. He's probably heard Mrs Matthews shouting for Abi. It's the only time you ever hear them, when Abi's playing them up. Little monkey that one's turning into. I don't know where she gets it

109

from. Not her Mam and Dad, that's for sure.

For the rest of the weekend Mark haunted the hotel and its grounds, leaving only when he'd seen the guests disappear on more organised outings and checked the time of their return. And always, he was aware of the packets of drugs lying useless as gold sovereigns in his inside pocket where there should have been cash to help him through the next few weeks.

Once or twice he caught sight of the Kells but each time they vanished before he could reach them. Playing games with him, that's what they were doing and what's more they were winning. But he'd find out what was happening, one way or another.

That young waiter chap would be serving them and Mark had seen the way Mrs Kell mothered him so it was quite likely Kevin had picked up some information. On the last morning of the holiday Mark hovered near the kitchen door that always stood open to allow fresh air into the overheated room.

As Kevin came in and out, delivering orders and collecting laden trays, there was a speed and a rhythm to his work that allowed no time for idle chat and Mark realised it was going to be hard to catch his attention. However, just as he was about to give up there was a smash of broken china and voices raised in anger towards one of the young workers. Like a flash Kevin crossed the kitchen to pick up another bowl. He passed the open door and with one hand, Mark grabbed him.

'What the hell?' Kevin gasped.

'Shut it,' Mark said and raised his free hand to show a lighted cigarette. Fear made Kevin's eyes bright and he kept very still. 'You serving the Kells this morning?'

Kevin's nod was the merest movement. The cigarette end glowed sharply between thick fingers. 'Find out what's happening to that son of theirs. I'll be back here in fifteen minutes.' Without a backward glance Mark walked away.

110

Kevin picked up a clean bowl and went on with his work as though nothing had happened, but inside he was shaking. Before he collected his next tray and pushed his way through the swing doors to the dining room he glanced at the clock that dominated the lives of the chef and his ever-changing staff. By seven minutes past, Kevin had to have his information. Not much time to serve all his tables and broach a difficult subject as well, but it would have to be done. As always the light and noise of the dining room cheered him. Leaving the Kells till last he made sure his other guests had all they needed then he approached his favourite couple.

'We were beginning to think you'd forgotten us,' Mr Kell said and his wife looked worried.

'Sorry sir. There was a bit of a disaster in the kitchen - - '

'It's alright dear.' Mrs Kell added. 'Tomorrow we'll have to get our own breakfast.' She made a wry face and Kevin took his opportunity, hoping nobody would overhear and accuse him of quizzing the guests.

'Will your son be home today as well?' he said and tried to smile and ignore the hard look on Mr Kell's face.

Mrs Kell gave her husband a warning glance then said 'No dear. Simon needs more care than we can manage now. But we go to see him every day . . . '

'I'm sorry. I didn't mean to be personal.'

'It's alright. Just you get on with your work.' Mr Kell dismissed him and Kevin was thankful to escape. But he kept away from the kitchen door until the last moment and then passed on the information briefly under the pretence of collecting clean crockery. He did not allow himself to wonder why Mark needed to know about the lives of any of the guests or what the repercussions were likely to be. It was enough that he'd delivered the message and escaped unharmed.

Later in the day when Mr Kell moved his Mercedes from the car park near the pool to the main front door, Mark was still

111

there, hovering round corners and attempting to be inconspicuous amongst the departing crowd. He felt certain that the other man had seen him by the way he packed their discreet black suitcases into the depth of the boot and carefully locked it before going into the hotel to shepherd his wife to the car and then actually lock her in before walking round to the other side and letting himself into the driver's seat.

No longer caring whether he was seen Mark stepped out into the middle of the drive to watch them until they disappeared on to the main road. Then he began to walk in the same direction with a step that did not vary although the moisture that had hung in the air all morning now turned to uncompromising rain and every car that passed sprayed water up to his knees.

Losing the licence was a worse punishment than anybody realised. He'd not only lost his official livelihood he'd lost his unofficial one as well. Wheeling and dealing in quiet lay-bys had become a way of life to him. Now his place would have been taken by some other driver who was eager to make an extra income. Mark would have to look nearer home.

Chapter Twenty-Three.

Mark stood near the window and watched the postman make his slow way along the road. He thought how strange it was that he'd never noticed the man before. He couldn't always have been away from home when the post arrived. Now he wondered how many hours the postman worked, what time he started in the morning and how far he tramped each day. Most of all Mark wondered if there were any vacancies and how *he* could apply for one. To work a definite route again would be something, even though it was walking instead of driving. It was still movement and purpose, delivering a load and coming back empty. There was satisfaction in that. A job well done. A wage at the end of the week.

Mark opened the door and stood on the step breathing in the clean morning air. If he worked in a city, he guessed the air would be polluted wherever he stood. He hated that` idea. Now he held out his hand to take the letter that was being offered and return the man's cheery greeting.

'Morning mate. Nearly finished, are you?'

The postman slapped the side of his sack. 'Bit to do yet,' he said. 'But it's a nice morning for it.' He went on his way and Mark watched till he'd passed his Mam's house without touching the shining brass letter box. Then Mark examined his own letter and gave a satisfied smile when he saw the brewery's logo in dark brown ink that reminded him of the colour of John Smith's ale. He could be pulling pints like that in a week or two's time. A bit of training and a certificate to hang behind the bar, then his name painted above the door of a busy pub in one of the market towns. *Landlord - Mark Wyburn.* It had a ring to it.

He tore at a corner of the envelope until there was enough space to put his finger inside and run it along, slitting the paper neatly and allowing the letter to slide out undamaged. Then he unfolded it, spreading it in both hands and noting how the logo was repeated on the heading. At last he allowed his eyes to drop to the precise message below. In a split second he'd crumpled the paper in one hand and flung it towards the empty fireplace where it bounced against the fret and fell back on to the cracked tiles of the hearth. Bastard conviction! It wasn't as though he was intending to drive. Why the hell did they think he wanted to live in a town? They could stuff their job. He wouldn't work for them if they begged him to.

* * * * *

Having Mark at home changed Donna's routine so that it was difficult for her to do her housework. She knew he did his best, but she would be thankful when he was working again. She'd heard him talking to the postman and went through to the front room to see if there'd been a letter for him, but he'd disappeared. She wondered if he'd gone along to his Mam's house to read it and she felt really annoyed until she noticed the crumpled paper lying on the hearth. When she straightened it out she understood why he'd walked away.

"We regret we cannot consider you for this post because of your recent Drink/Driving conviction."

Donna thought they should have expected it but all the same she'd liked the idea of a pub. There'd have been heaps of space for the four of them - their own house seemed to have shrunk since Mark was here all the time.

Rumour had it that Mrs Matthews was finding her flat too small as well now that she had two children to cope with. But Donna envied her - there would be no shortage of money there and they could easily afford a house in the village. Donna could see one now from her own bedroom window. She might casually mention it to Sarah so that she could pass the message on.

114

* * * * *

As Mark walked he thought of Andrew Matthews running that big hotel. No convictions against *him* of course. Never put a foot wrong in his whole life, he could bet on that but all he had to do was put a good face on and smile at the guests. Anybody could do that! The only trouble he'd ever had was when his wife left him and then she'd come back after a few days, so it hardly counted. Then of course Camilla being born disabled was a nasty knock for anybody and a problem that wasn't going to go away. Mark knew he should be thankful that these extra children of his had slotted so easily into the Matthews' lives, but he wasn't. He wanted to earn enough to keep them in style. And he wanted Donna to know and to forgive him. But he couldn't do any of that and his life was sliding downhill at an incredible speed.

It looked as though Donna was right after all and the best thing would be to try for a factory job. But he was damned if he would stay with Renee and her husband. He'd rather be in the Salvation Army hostel and that was saying something. He'd have to get extra money somehow. He knew there'd always be somebody ready for a bit of dealing, but another idea was forming in his mind and the thought of how it was going to upset Helen Matthews put him in a better mood for the rest of the day.

* * * * *

For the next few weeks Mark made it his business to discover when room 83 was unoccupied. He chuckled to himself when he remembered how easy it had been to have a duplicate key cut. He'd only had to study Sarah's routine for a few days to realise that she left the desk in the middle of every morning and every afternoon, for just long enough to make coffee. The guests were already launched into their day's programme so that the reception area was empty.

Timing it to perfection, he shot behind the desk and grabbed the key from its peg, replacing it with the one for number thirty-three. At a quick glance they could easily be confused and 83's empty peg was not so noticeable in the middle of a line of full ones.

By the middle of the afternoon Mark had had it copied. A bright new key lay in his pocket and the old one was dangling on its heavy ring on the last peg in the line. Sarah drank her coffee, blissfully unaware that anything had happened.

Now he simply had to pass reception to see the key hanging there and know that the room was unoccupied. Once he'd opened the door and found somebody else's belongings there and he'd backed out quickly, chuckling about how she'd feel if she knew he had access to the room, but he had no interest in the cheap jewellery or the highly scented toiletries that filled the shelf round the ancient bath.

He only wanted the window and the view across the yard to the Matthews' flat. He would stretch comfortably on the bed while he learnt the routine of the family opposite. He knew the times they went for walks and the times that they drove off in the car. And he knew the times that Abi played outside, wheeling her dolls in a double pushchair or careering round the yard on a little green tractor that Lewis would love to have owned if only he'd known it existed. He also knew that occasionally Helen popped back inside and the children were alone for just a minute or two.

Sometimes Camilla sat in her chair by the open door, but without the activity of playing she soon became cold and had to be cocooned in blankets. Mark always felt uneasy when she was there, sensing that she might see him through the flimsy net curtain and indicate his presence in some speechless way. Something about her determination reminded him of his mother and he knew she would be a survivor.

116

I don't know what's come over our Mark. He's looking pleased with himself but when I ask him where he goes he just shrugs his shoulders and says, "Out and about."

I don't expect him to stay with us all day but he could be here sometimes. As it is, he picks Charlie up from school and they come in together. It must be me he doesn't want although he's all over me when he is here.

I tell myself he's used to the roads and being away for days at a time. It'll not be easy for him, but he should be applying for one of those jobs.

He had this idea of being a postman and it would have suited him but it turned out he'd have to get himself to the sorting office about four o'clock in the morning and without a car . . .

It was a black day when he discovered that.

Mark squatted next to Camilla. The fine mist of the morning had given way to sunshine that dried the ground in a surprisingly short time. With one hand he reached up and knocked a toy that was securely suctioned on to her table, making it rock madly from side to side so that the balls inside whirled in a riot of colour and the child laughed in a remarkably normal way. Abi wheeled her pram towards him in an amazing imitation of her mother. 'Again,' she said as the bright balls settled back into place.

Mark touched the toy with a stubby forefinger. He neither smiled nor spoke but the children laughed in delight at the novelty of his company.

'What's going on?' Helen appeared at the door, sensing the change in the girls' voices and peeling rubber gloves off as she came. 'What the devil are you doing here?' she demanded, grabbing Camilla's chair and releasing the brake so that she could turn it towards the front door. 'Inside, Abi. Now!' she ordered as the child hesitated but Mark was ahead of her,

117

positioning himself across the open doorway. Above them a single gull screeched from the roof top.

'Move,' she said, 'or I get the police.'

He shrugged his shoulders. 'I'm their father. I have my rights.'

'That's not what you said at the time.'

'Times change. Anybody can see they're Wyburns.'

'Don't cause trouble now. You didn't want to know then. You can't start now.'

'What's it worth?'

'Money? Is that what this's about?'

'How much. To keep things sweet?'

'I can't pay you . . .'

'You're rolling in it.'

'Andrew is. I'm not.'

'I'll ask him then.'

'No.' She put one arm round Abi's shoulders and drew the child to her.

'You've got two days to decide.'

Helen watched him cross the Stable Yard and disappear round the edge of the Grooms' cottages. Abi ran inside but Helen stood there, tightening her grip on the wheelchair and remembering how angry Andrew had been when application forms had come for posts in London and Birmingham. How he'd blamed Sarah for it until the girl had handed in her notice and threatened to make a formal complaint. Then Helen had confessed and he hadn't spoken to her for a week, muttering about "undermining my position" and "redundancy."

It was only recently that they'd settled into an uneasy truce that certainly wouldn't survive Mark Wyburn's intervention. In spite of Andrew's failings Helen appreciated the life-style he provided for them and was shrewd enough to realise that it would be difficult to manage without him.

Later that afternoon she parked her car by the nearest

118

cash-point. With shaking fingers she punched in the identifying code and waited for her balance to appear on the murky screen. As a double check she requested a mini-statement and took it back to the car to mull over the figures in private. Her monthly allowance was there as usual, transferred from Andrew's account with unfailing regularity. Rarely mentioned but taken for granted that it would cover food and all the usual household expenses. Other bills were paid as they arrived and Helen had no need to consider them.

The black figures at the bottom of the slip showed a healthy credit but she knew that every penny would be needed to see her through the remaining three weeks. No matter how she tried, she'd never been able to save anything. There was always some unforeseen expense and while Andrew expected his family to be a credit to him he would not tolerate extravagance. Helen remembered the days when she'd had her own income and had happily squandered a week's wages on a single outfit. She sighed and concentrated on the figures before her.

If the girls could wait till next month, for new sandals, she could offer that money to Mark. It wasn't a lot but he hadn't quoted any definite figure and it might mollify him for the moment. Donna had told her he was looking for work, so things could soon improve.

In the back of the car Abi slapped Camilla, and she gave an angry cry, but Helen ignored them both and went back to collect £50 from her account and put it carefully in the front pocket of her bag.

* * * * *

'Fifty quid! You're joking aren't you?' Mark said as Helen held out two £20 notes and a £10 one.
'I told you - I don't have much.'
'Don't give me that. Look at the car you're driving.'
'But I don't pay for it.'

119

'He'll give you running costs.'

'I have to show him the receipts,' she said sheepishly.

Mark snorted and flung his head back. 'I'll need double that.'

'I can't . . .'

'It's up to you. I'll be back.'

'I might manage seventy.'

He nodded. 'For this time.'

Chapter Twenty-Four.

Paul Hutchinson watched the rain lashing against the dining-room window, leaving rivulets of water that snaked down the glass and settled against the metal frame, only to be replaced by others until the whole pane was a writhing mass of water and the guests made disgruntled comments as they planned their Spring Bank Holiday. If he'd felt like talking he would have asked why they'd come to the Lake District when all they wanted was sunshine.

These were fair-weather people, not dedicated walkers like he used to be. He had no patience with them and showed it by getting up from the table and pushing his way past the queue of latecomers waiting to collect their cereals and fruit juice. One or two smiled and made way with a friendly word or two but he didn't respond as he limped back to his room to listen to the radio and cast on a new piece of knitting.

He would use green wool this time and a few strands of yellow to remind him of the daffodils growing wild by the edge of the lakes where the darkness of the trees met the lighter shades of the fields. A few years ago he would have gloried in a wet day like this, tramping the paths and appreciating the freshness of the countryside.

Instead, two new pieces of knitting lay neatly folded in the bottom of his sports bag and he expected to complete three or four more before the week was over. Everybody asked what he was making but it was none of their business and he wouldn't give them the satisfaction of knowing that some day he would have a glorious new bedcover showing all the colours of the Lake District. Not only the obvious greens and blues of hills and water but the small things - the black of a sheep's face, the subtle colour of a duck's wing as it flapped it dry above the water. Bright colours that represented tourists' clothes and dark brown like the hiking boots they wore. Then there were all the natural shades of the flowers in the parks that he used to pass so quickly on his way to the hills. To an untrained eye the bedcover would be a hotchpotch of colour, but to him it would represent a lifetime's pleasure and he would recognise every inch of it.

A sudden movement outside made him look up. He'd chosen this room for its privacy and its view into the partially shaded garden. Now he resented the intrusion of another human being but presumed somebody was taking a short cut because of the incessant rain. When the figure materialised into Mark Wyburn Paul reached out with one of his knitting needles until he could just touch the window. Then he knocked hard on the glass with its circular metal end, but the noise was muffled by the double glazing and Mark passed without a glance.

Paul levered himself down from his chair and limped along the corridor to the outside door and the steps that led down in two directions. Ignoring the ones to the hotel he hobbled down those that went straight into the stable yard, then he stopped short at the sight of Mark standing outside the manager's flat and obviously in heated conversation with Mrs Matthews. Paul could have sworn the man's foot was wedged in the doorway and certainly she seemed to be trying to close the door. A child appeared at the window, smiled in recognition and waved a friendly greeting that Mark acknowledged with a movement of his own hand. Mrs Matthew moved back and for a moment it seemed as though Mark would force his way in but the door came forward again and she was there, jerking her head in angry conversation until Mark left. His head was high and every movement declared him the winner.

Paul pressed himself into the shadow of the building and Mark strode past without seeing him. His eyes were fixed on the road ahead and the Mercedes car that was unmistakeably, the Kells. As Paul turned back into the building and the comfort of his own room he wondered what connection there could possibly

122

be between a rough man like Mark Wyburn and a business-man like Mr Kell. Something shady was going on there or his name wasn't Paul Hutchinson.

Typical Bank Holiday weather. You can't see the hills at all so it'll probably not lift and we'll be cooped up in here as usual. But one day's just like another now with Mark mooching about like a lost soul. He's out already - heaven only knows where he's gone and he certainly won't tell me when he comes back.

And the hotel's booked solid - except for 83 and nobody wants a room without a shower these days. The Kells are here again, but they're keeping well away from me and she used to make such a fuss. I feel awful about it. I wonder if it's something I said but I can't think what. Then there's poor Mr Hutchinson sitting by himself all the time. And all that knitting he does - it's not natural. I'm going to make a point of speaking to him and see if I can get him out of his shell a bit.

As the week on the weather improved until a few of the hardiest were able to sit at the tables in the garden, but Paul was the only one who settled there for any length of time. People nodded or stopped for a moment to exchange a few polite words then went on with the business of their own holiday, satisfied that they'd done their duty by the one single guest in the hotel.

If there were times when Paul resented his position he was too proud to show it and as the week went by his knitting grew and he could begin to plan the way he would piece it together when he got back home. With another square completed he laid down his needles and took a sketching pad from the bag at his feet. With coloured pencils he began to shade in the patterns. Time and again he gave up one idea and turned the page to start again, with utmost patience. So absorbed was he, that when a

123

friendly hand was laid on his shoulder he was startled out of all proportion.

'You're an artist as well, are you?' It was Donna on her way to start the evening shift.

'Can be.' In his surprise he forgot to be unpleasant.

'Lovely colours. Mind if I look?'

He pushed the pad to the side of the table where she could see it better. 'It's the Lake District I remember from my walking days. The knitting's going to be a bedcover . . .' Afterwards, he never could understand why he'd confided in her, but there was concern in her voice and a warmth about her that he suddenly realised he'd been missing for a very long time.

She pointed to a particularly soft grey. 'That's the colour of the hills in the morning before the mist lifts, isn't it?'

Paul nodded then rubbed his finger across a soft shade of pink. '"Pink sky in the morning, shepherd's warning." I've seen a few of those in my time.' He was talking almost to himself. 'I can't walk the hills any more but it doesn't mean I have to forget.'

She patted his shoulder again. 'Of course it doesn't. You're a very brave man.'

Overcome with emotion, she suddenly kissed his cheek and walked away. Paul watched her disappear towards the kitchen, then he put his hand up to his face. He couldn't think how long it was since anybody had kissed him and he wondered if it might have been safer to stay that way. He picked up a pencil the colour of bright sunlight and began to shade in the very centre of the page.

Chapter Twenty-Five.

Mark sat at a wooden table outside the cafe that flanked one side of the bus station. It was a quiet place, even at 5 o'clock on a Saturday afternoon when day trippers were preparing to leave the quaint little town where market-stalls filled the centre of the road and vied for business with the shops on either side.

His coffee cup had been empty for some time but he sat on, watching for the only bus of the week that would take him all the way to Durham City. A Summer-Saturday special that took all morning to arrive and all evening to drive back, but had the distinct advantage of being cheap.

When Mrs Monaghan had told every customer who came into the post office, that her family were visiting from Wednesday to Saturday, Mark had been quick to ask for a lift as far as Keswick, even though it meant arriving at lunch-time and filling in the afternoon with aimless wanderings until he hated the very sight of tourists, especially the ones who were obviously enjoying themselves and he regretted the night when he'd drunk so much alcohol that it had stayed in his blood till the next morning. If he could have turned the clock back everything would have been different.

Now he watched a small group of people congregating at one of the open bus stands. Today, it been had warm enough for him to take his jacket off and stuff it into the sports bag that contained enough clothes for the coming week. Donna had arranged for him to stay overnight with her mother, which meant he would join her at the club where she spent every Saturday night with the group of friends she'd known for years. There would be noise and laughter and he would fit easily into the crowd as though he was one of the regulars. Tomorrow he would make his way to Sunderland where Renee would have a room ready for him. It would be clean and tidy with motoring magazines on the bedside table and a lamp within easy reach. Downstairs, they would welcome him into their atmosphere of educational television programmes relieved only by quizzes that he couldn't answer and didn't want to anyway. Their little girl would be well-behaved and he'd miss the fun of his own two boys.

As the single-decker bus drew towards the stand, Mark left the cafe and ambled across to join the queue. The bus was low, designed for easy access for wheelchairs or pushchairs but it was highly uncomfortable for the rest of the passengers. The only empty seat was a small tip-up one near the driver and before the deep step that led able-bodied people to more comfortable places at the back.

When Mark flipped the seat down and sat quickly on it, he found that the back-rest was stiff and straight and certainly not meant for a long journey. Even with his height he could hardly see out of the window. When he fished in his pocket for cigarettes, a young mother pointed to the No-Smoking sign and twisted her pushchair away from him as though his very presence would contaminate her child.

As they made their way towards Penrith he stared up towards the tops of the hills and wondered whether he could ever bear to live anywhere else, even if he was lucky enough to find a job that would support them all.

Several passengers rose to their feet as the driver brought them expertly in to the bus station and Mark took his chance to move to a more comfortable seat where he could sit high and have the sort of view he was used to in his lorry. If he looked past the man sitting next to him he could see the fields that were dotted with sheep feeding on lush green grass.

'I'll swap if you like,' the man's voice broke in.

'You're alright, mate. I can see from here.'

'Have it if you like. I'm here every Saturday, wet or fine.'

126

Mark glared at him but refrained from saying that it was only the bus that was new to him. The road was as familiar as the back of his hand.

Now as he paid more attention to his neighbour he cursed himself for choosing this seat. The discomfort of the first one had probably been preferable to the boredom that was ahead of him. The man was middle-aged but wearing his hair in a pony-tail that settled on to the collar of his blue denim jacket. He was pulling a canvas bag on to his knee and he brought out a yellow container with an advertisement for butter just discernible on the shabby sides. 'There's two pieces of chocolate cake left. I'm always hungry on the way back,' he said.

When he removed the lid a piece of well-used grease-proof paper rested on top of the cake and the man took it between finger and thumb and put it on the upturned lid in what was obviously a weekly ritual. Then to Mark's surprise he produced a kitchen roll decorated with green leaves and tore one sheet from it then handed it to Mark.

'You'll need that, it's crumbly,' he said.

'I don't want your cake . . '

'You will when you taste it. Melts in your mouth. I make one every Thursday to bring on the Saturday.'

'You're on your own then?'

'I am and happy that way. What about you?'

'Family man myself.'

'Oh?' It was definitely a question and as Mark bit into the cake he began to talk. After all the man was a stranger and once the journey was over they would go their separate ways without even exchanging names.

'I've got the best wife in the lake district and two little lads. The youngest's not at school yet.'

The man chuckled. 'So you're having a weekend on your own are you?'

'Not the way you mean. I'm job hunting.'

127

'Ah right. Not much work over here then?'

'You could say that. I'm going to the wife's people for a week to see if I can find anything there. A factory job or something. Donna would like to be back . . .'

'I gather you wouldn't'

'Not if it means lodging with her sister and I might have to till we got sorted. Couldn't afford two rents, you know what I mean.'

'There's a spare room at my house . . .'

'You don't know me. I might be an axe murderer . . .'

'So might I, but I'm not and if I can be of any help . . .'

'I might take you up on that.' To Mark's surprise the man produced a printed card from his pocket.

'My details,' he said, 'if ever I can be of service. Incidentally, there are several factories near my home.'

With that, he gathered up the debris from the picnic and packed it neatly away, then he unfolded the Daily Telegraph and read it for the remainder of the journey.

When Mark checked the card later, in the cloakroom of the Workingmen's Club, he discovered the man was Roger Keogh and he lived in a new town near Sunderland. He could be a very useful connection.

Mark phoned up in the middle of the week. It sounds as if they're being really kind, getting lists of job vacancies for him and taking him round to find the agencies and job centres. But he says there's not a lot going and plenty of people after jobs. He's phoned round a few factories as well and two places are sending application forms out. It's going to be slow though so I hope he doesn't go and upset Renee. They hardly know each other and it won't be easy for any of them. He says he's coming home on Saturday. It'll just be for a few hours but it'll give them all a break.

Everybody at the hotel's being kind. Sarah took the boys

out for me on Sunday and even Mrs. Matthews seems interested,
wanting to know if Mark'll be home at the weekends. I told her
it would only be Saturdays, but she says she goes off with the
girls then. Well it'll be a long day for her with Mr Matthews busy
at the hotel and she has the car of course. She's lucky to have
that.

It was three Saturdays later that Mark had the first news of
a job. Donna guessed something had happened when she heard
him whistling as he walked towards the cottage. The previous
week he'd been very deflated, criticising everything and
snapping at the boys. As he'd set out for the awkward journey
back he'd muttered threats about staying in one place or the other
and not attempting this ridiculous Saturday visit that gave him no
more than a couple of hours with his own family. As for
wandering into the hotel grounds and contacting old friends, it
was simply out of the question and when Donna tried to keep
him up to date with the gossip, it seemed like another world to
him.

Now as he came into the living room, he picked Lewis up
and threw him towards the ceiling making the boy laugh with
delight. Then he fished in his pocket and brought out two
packets of candy-sticks and the children strutted round the room
pretending to smoke cigarettes.

'Oh Mark, the food's nearly ready . . .'

'Let them be. It'll give us a chance to go upstairs.' He
took her hand and moved towards the kitchen where the stairs
disappeared into a dark tunnel. 'Be good you two and I'll give
you something else when I come down.'

A short time later Donna and Mark lay back against the
pillows. Their bodies curved together in familiar pattern.

'You're beautiful, Donna. There's nobody to match you
over there.'

'Better not be either, Mark Wyburn. You're only looking
129

for a job, nothing else. And the sooner we're back together the better.'

'It shouldn't be long now.'

'Tell me then.'

'There's an interview set up for Monday at one of the places I phoned. They sent forms out. I filled them in and got them straight back.'

'They must like the sound of you then.'

'There's a lot of men going. They run tests - a bit of English and Maths and sorting shapes into patterns . . .'

'Are they wanting bosses, then?'

'No, but they're opening a new section where the work's all done with robots. They must want people with a bit about them. Can't be bad.'

'You'll cope alright. Nothing slow about you.' She laughed and wriggled away from him. 'Come on, those boys'll be hungry.'

* * * * *

Mark stared at the sheet of questions in front of him and tried to think back to schooldays. He'd spent most of his time aggravating the teachers so that his poor results had come as no surprise to anybody, however he must have absorbed some of the information and now he brought it from the depths of his mind and discovered that he knew most of the answers. He even had a few minutes at the end to take stock of the other candidates. The one nearest to him was a thin, determined lad with the unmistakable air of a schoolboy. As he laid his pen carefully back into its black case he turned a smug smile towards Mark.

Mark hoped he would never have to work next to him. Further forward, several men still struggled to complete the paper. Average men, nothing to single them out by their appearance, except for one - a big chap who would have seemed more in place standing outside a night club, preparing to break

130

up trouble as it began. As it was he shuffled on the hard chair and laid his pen down only when the order came from Fiona, the stylish young lady who was in charge of the whole procedure.

'You can have a ten minute break now,' she was saying, as she collected the last of the papers from another heavy man at the back of the room, 'but anybody who's late back will be disqualified.'

Mark headed for the outside door and the welcome fresh air. He thought how often he'd delivered loads to factories like this and how relieved he'd been when he'd driven away again. Yet here he was, doing his best to spend the next few years in just such a place. The idea of being one of the first to work on the robot project appealed to him, but a woman boss definitely did not.

The other men soon began to walk back in with the schoolboy three steps in front. 'Come on, you don't want to be disqualified,' he called out and grinned in a satisfied way.

Mark ignored him and nodded to the others.

Fiona was there already, her pin-striped trouser suit accentuating her femininity. 'This test will last for thirty-five minutes. No speaking from now on.'

'Excuse me?' The voice came from the back of the room. Mark couldn't see who it was, but he was as shocked as the rest of the group when the man was ordered to leave, disqualified from the test and losing the chance of a new start in life. A hush descended on the room. The men stared at their papers and the peculiar shapes that were meant to fit into some sort of pattern.

To Mark it was easy. Upside down or sideways, the right shape was always there and he could see exactly how it would complete the picture. He finished while most people still had half their questions to do. As he stared round the room Fiona came forward and bent over him to whisper, 'Why have you stopped?'

'Finished,' he said and the scent of her perfume wafted

131

round him in sensual waves. He couldn't identify it. It wasn't one that Donna used. But whatever it was, it was having a serious effect on him and the idea of her being in charge became more appealing by the minute. He forced his eyes away from her, afraid that his feelings would be too obvious.

The boy next to him was busy with his last question but Mark could see a space at the top of the paper where he'd forgotten to write his name. Mark smiled and made no attempt to catch his attention.

When it was all over and they filed out again Mark kept his distance as he'd done before. They were strangers. They might never meet again and if they did, that was time enough to get to know each other. He wouldn't waste his efforts now.

When they were called back in Fiona announced without preamble, 'I want the following three people to stay. The rest of you can leave. Thank you.'

Mark was one to stay and he was thankful to see that the boy was not. The bouncer look-alike *was* and the big man from the back.

'You will be given an appointment for a medical examination and all being well, will begin work on the first of the month. Welcome to the company and good luck.' Fiona left the room with a toss of her stylish head. A hint of a smile played around her lips.

'He's got it,' I say the minute I see Sarah. I cleaned the rooms in double quick time this morning. Even dusted the tops of the wardrobes and I've been singing all the way round.

Sarah laughs. 'I knew something had happened. You're not usually this cheerful in a morning.'

I dance a little jig with the vacuum cleaner. I'm going to live near Renee. I'm going back home. The boys'll grow up in my part of the world, not in this horrible place where it's always raining and everything's a long way away because you have to get right round to the other side of the lake.

'Have you told Mr Matthews yet?'

'No. Well I'll have to wait a bit. It's a twelve week trial at first. But Mark's a good worker, he'll be alright.'

'D'you think he'll settle? It's a big change from driving.'

'He's over the moon. Only three of them got jobs out of a whole roomful, you know.'

'He must be good then, Donna. I didn't realise . . .'

I try to hide my anger. Sarah's a good girl and she's helped with the boys such a lot since Mark went away. 'You have to be bright, to cope with long-distance driving,' I say, 'but I'm glad he's finished with that. He'll be home every night, depending on the shifts, you know.'

'It'll be lovely. I'm really pleased for you, Donna. But I'll miss you.'

'You can be our first visitor. And bring Kevin across as well. You'll have space in the car.'

Donna dreamt of the house they would have. They'd be able to buy one now with a garden and a climbing frame. She would grow roses on the fence, and lupins and hollyhocks against the garage wall and a few sunflowers for the boys to look after. They would have a spare room for visitors and Mark would invite his Mam for a weekend when he wasn't working. Donna knew they had to wait twelve weeks, but it didn't mean they couldn't look, did it?

'Where will you be living exactly?' Sarah was asking.

'Somewhere near the factory. He's going to lodge with a man over there at first. It's the only way he'll get in on time.'

'As long as *you* like it . . .'

'I'll like it. Anywhere without in-laws'll do for me.'

'Mark'll have them though, won't he?'

'Sh. Don't mention it. He might never realise and they won't be in the same street, will they?'

133

Chapter Twenty Six.

By half past eight Andrew had gone to the office and
Helen knew that she wouldn't see him again until the children
were in bed for the night. The day stretched ahead of her with
awful emptiness and worse still, with the threat of Mark's
appearance in a few hours' time. Pride forbade her from
enquiring about his whereabouts, but it was sensible to leave
both the hotel and the village until the danger had passed.

Abi was already rushing round the stable yard on her
tractor and already demanding that Camilla should be placed
beside her, as a captive audience. Helen was beginning to realise
just how much Camilla resented being strapped into a wheelchair
when she wanted to run and jump and play just as much as Abi
did. Even now she was shaking her head and making it obvious
that she did *not* want to be taken outside to sit and watch.

Helen stood in the hall and saw her trying to balance a red
plastic cup with a lid and a spout, towards her ever-moving
mouth whilst Abi made her demands very clear indeed. Helen
sighed and wanted to burst into tears. Instead she grabbed her
keys and hurried out to unlock the car.

'We'll have a day away, Abi,' she said. 'Come off the
tractor now.'

A few minutes later when Helen struggled to get Camilla
in to her special seat Abi was still pedalling round with ceaseless
energy.

'Quickly, Abi. We're going.'
'No.'
'Yes, jump in the back.'
'Don't want to.'
'Yes you do. You know you do.'
'I want the front.'

Helen dumped two large bags bulging with spare clothes
134

and toys, into the boot and slammed the lid down as Abi circled round again. Helen resisted the temptation to jump into the car and drive away - anywhere that was far from children and toys and hotels on Saturdays. Instead she strode across to Abi and heaved her forcibly from the tractor. Ignoring the child's flailing legs and screams of protest, she managed to open the passenger door with one hand and dump Abi on to the front seat with the other, quickly clicking the seat-belt into place. Abi gave a satisfied grin while Helen went to her own side and turned the key viciously in the ignition.

The car leapt forward. Helen kept her foot hard on the throttle. They shrieked past the steps to the Grooms' Cottages and swerved round the corner on to the main drive. The lawn was decorated with balloons and bunting and Helen remembered that Andrew expected her to make an appearance at the Church Fayre that was being held in the hotel grounds that afternoon. She swung the steering wheel violently to the right. She would stop at the office for a moment and let him know she was leaving. He would be furious but she didn't care. At least she was telling him and he could make some excuse for his family's absence. The thought of being polite to all those people was more than she could bear and yet she knew the children would love every minute of it and be the centre of everybody's attention.

Deep in thought, she never saw the dark Mercedes that was approaching from the opposite direction and afterwards Mr Kell could not remember exactly how many seconds he'd had to try to stop the car and avoid the crash that had embedded the front of *his* car into the passenger side of Helen's. He only knew that the sound of the crash and the sight of the child's blood would live with him for ever. Helen's screams sent shivers through his whole body, but Abi's silence was more unnerving still.

Everybody hears the crash. It's breakfast time so they're all going into the dining room and it happens just outside. Kevin tells me that Mrs Kell's been there for a few minutes, at their usual table near the window. She's waiting for her husband, but he's driven down to the post office to buy the Saturday Times that they always order for him. She can see his car coming back through the grounds and he's just going to turn towards the main door when Mrs Matthew's car appears. Just out of nowhere, he says. Then Bang. The two cars are locked together.

Mrs Matthews is screaming and we can see the blood even from here. Kevin doesn't know which of the twins is hurt, but he knows it isn't Mr Kell's fault. Anyway, Mrs Kell jumps up from the table and bolts for the door. On the way she catches hold of Mr Matthews' hand and pulls him along with her.

'An accident,' she shouts. 'It's your wife's car and the children are in with her.'

Andrew raced outside while Kevin dashed to the nearest phone and rang 999. The guests crowded to the window, leaving their breakfast to go cold on the tables. Some were in tears, until Mr Kell got out of his car then a sigh of relief went round the whole room.

They watched Mr Matthews attempting to calm his wife then going round to the passenger side, but the door seemed to be jammed. However the ambulance was already screaming through the grounds. Donna hurried out to see if she could help and Mrs Matthews sent a beseeching look towards her as one of the paramedics guided her towards the ambulance. Donna would never forget that look as long as she lived. Once Mrs Matthews had gone it was easy for them to reach over to the little girl and deal with her and while they were doing that Mr Matthews managed to open the back door of the car and lift the other twin out. She was crying very quietly and he handed her straight to

136

Donna.

'Take care of her, Donna,' he said and turned back to the car.

As Donna cuddled the child close to her she realised that it was Camilla and for a split second she wished it had been Abi. But she quickly squashed that idea and took Camilla into the hotel. She didn't have a key to the flat so she had to take her to her own home even though she knew Mark would be coming later.

* * * * *

'If you'd like to wait in the relatives' room, doctor'll be with you soon,' the nurse said. Her straight fair hair and pale face gave the appearance of a schoolgirl but her uniform showed she was a fully qualified nurse. He could only pray that she was capable of saving Abi's life.

'We should be with her . . . my wife . . .'

'Your wife's still being checked over. They'll bring her here as soon as she's ready.'

'But Abi needs her mother . . .'

'Abi's not conscious yet. When she comes round she'll want you both.'

'Will she be alright?' Beyond the door, muted footsteps padded along the corridor and a trolley rattled as it was wheeled to a cubicle. Was Helen on it? Was *she* alright? The future that had seemed so secure, now stretched into murky darkness.

'It's too early to say. She's lost a lot of blood,' the nurse was saying, 'but doctor'll talk to you as soon as they've got her stabilised.' She left the room, presumably to return to Abi - such a scrap of humanity she'd seemed when they laid her on the stretcher opposite her mother. So strangely immobile and unresponsive when they'd spoken to her.

Andrew sat on a hard chair. Striped curtains billowed at the open window and a Coke machine dominated one corner. If

137

the news proved to be bad he would rather not hear it in a room like this and certainly not alone. He wondered if there was time to track down Helen in one of the departments connected with Accident and Emergency, but decided against it. At least she was adult and able to reason for herself whereas Abi . . .

Poor Abi. What had she been doing in the front seat? He'd bought the most expensive baby seats for the back of the car and always insisted that the girls were strapped into them before the engine was switched on, yet she hadn't been this time. How many more times had Helen defied him? What was she thinking of? Did she not know how much his children meant to him?

When the door opened and Helen appeared in a wheelchair pushed by one of the porters Andrew was too angry to care that she was wearing a surgical collar or that her face was whiter than the bandage on her left wrist.

'She might die,' he charged her. 'Do you know that?

Helen nodded her head. 'Yes,' she whispered, 'and it'll be my fault for being in a temper.'

'You were in a temper?'

'She wouldn't get in the car. Just wanted to ride that tractor, round and round and round . . .'

'If she dies I'll never forgive you.'

'What if I'd died?'

His silence was answer enough and she guessed that he was praying but was not sure what he was asking for. It was a relief when the doctor arrived.

'Ah, Mrs Matthews, it's good to see you're back with us. Abi's asking for you.'

'She's conscious then?' Andrew asked.

'Is she going to be alright?' Helen's eyes were anxious.

'I think so. She's very weak and she's lost a lot of blood so we've set up a transfusion for her. Very unusual blood group,

138

B negative but of course, you'll know that. One of you must be the same.'

Chapter Twenty-Seven.

Donna's arms ached before she'd carried Camilla even as far as Reception. She'd simply gone to collect her things and leave a message with Sarah in case Mr Matthews needed to know where Camilla was. She could see through to the dining room where the guests were all back at their own tables. She couldn't hear what they were saying but she guessed they were not talking about the accident any more. Just getting on with their own lives. Nobody had died and the excitement was all over.

Kevin was bringing out fresh coffee and jugs of hot water, making sure his tables had everything they needed. He was a real treasure, Donna decided. She'd seen several apprentices but he beat them all. She caught his eye and he waved but he was too busy to speak to her.

Sarah switched on a tape and music floated around the landings and all the main rooms. Donna hated that classical stuff, but the guests must have liked it because they never complained.

'Give me a bit of good jazz any day of the week,' she would say, but nevertheless she found herself moving to the rhythm and when she looked down Camilla was fast asleep. She was much heavier than she looked and it was a long walk to the village. Donna was tempted to ring for a taxi and charge it to Mr Matthews, but if he refused to pay she couldn't afford to.

She sat down for a minute on a chair by the door, just beside the picture-postcard rack. She was thinking how lovely Camilla looked when she was asleep, so peaceful and calm you wouldn't think there was anything the matter with her at all, when Mr Hutchinson stopped beside her. He must have seen her from the garden and come over. He was such a nice man, Donna couldn't understand why he was alone so much.

'You'll need her wheelchair,' he said. 'You can't be carrying her all the way home.'

'It'll be in the boot of the car though,' Donna said. 'We won't be able to get it.'

'There's ways and means, you know. Ways and means.' He thought of all the accidents he'd attended as a Paramedic and the difficult situations he'd had to cope with in those days. As Donna laid Camilla on a dark red sofa and put her jacket over her Paul Hutchinson went to Mrs Matthews' car. He went straight to the boot and tried to open it but it wouldn't budge. Donna simply shook her head. However he tried the driver's door and found that it wasn't locked. Donna watched him lean inside the car and touch something. Then she heard a click and the boot lid moved the least bit.

'That's got it,' he said and came to the back of the car and lift it high, revealing a boot packed tight with toys and food and odds and ends that looked as though they'd been there for ever. And underneath it all was the blue and white wheelchair. Donna was so relieved that she felt like crying but instead she gave Mr Hutchinson a big hug as he pulled it out and set it up on the drive beside her.

'Steady on,' he grunted.

'You're a genius,' she said. 'Knowing how to do that.'

'It's nothing.'

Mr Hutchinson looks pleased and I guess he doesn't get many chances of helping other people.

'D'you want to walk over with me and have a cup of coffee? Mark won't be coming for a few hours yet and I can collect the boys from his Mam's as we go in.'

He turns a funny shade of pink. He's blushing. 'No,' he says. 'Haven't time. The taxi's coming for me at half past.'

'You're going home, are you?' I don't know why I should feel disappointed but I do.

141

'Fraid so. But I'll be back . . . at the end of July.'
'That's quick. You must like us here.' I laugh.
'I do,' he says. 'Oh yes, I do.'

Mark closed the front door and stared at the small wheelchair that Charlie was pushing through the overcrowded living-room. Camilla was flopping to one side and Lewis was squashed in beside her, both laughing and looking remarkably alike.

'Hello sunshine,' he said as the chair came to a stop in front of him. 'Where's that sister of yours? Hiding in the kitchen, is she?'

'She's in hospital . . .' Charlie said.

'Yes, hospital.' The boys were excited, quick to tell the news.

'Donna.' Mark charged into the kitchen then over to the stairs. 'Donna, where are you? What's going on?'

A few minutes later he dialled the hospital number and Donna listened in amazement as he made enquiries at one department after another until he finally traced Abi to the right ward. Living away from home had changed him, she thought. Being chosen for the new job had given him a confidence that he hadn't had before. Life was going to be better in the future. She could sense it. And they would be living in a town again. She smiled and stood close beside him.

'Fuck them.' He slammed the phone down. 'As comfortable as can be expected.' What the hell does that mean?'

'You're not a relative . . .'

'Am I not? We've got her twin sister. We should know what's going on.'

He pulled a stool out from under the table and slumped on to it. A pan boiled over on the old cooker behind him and Donna lifted the lid and stirred something inside. Then she made a mug of coffee from the blue kettle that simmered beside it and passed

142

it to Mark. He picked it up and carried it to the doorway where he could watch the three children playing so happily together.

'I'm going to find out,' he said a few minutes later and put the half-empty mug back on the kitchen table. 'There's a train due. I'll just catch it.'

'But you'll miss your bus back . . .'

He was gone, running along the road past the post office where Mrs Monaghan was engaged in her never ending gossip. Past the main drive to the Ascot hotel and then past the little wicket gate that led to the twisting footpath through the trees and up towards the pool. The level crossing gates were closed and the train screeched as it appeared round the bend in the track. Mark leapt on to the platform and into a carriage, the doors banged shut and the train pulled away.

Abi might die and he'd never see her again. She was more of a Wyburn than any of them were and yet he couldn't claim her. He drummed his fingers against the window until the man opposite frowned pointedly at him.

'Got a problem?' Mark said and the man turned away.

As the train approached the station Mark moved towards the door and was the first to jump on to the platform as it pulled to a halt. The £10 note in his pocket was meant to last the whole weekend, but he walked straight to the taxi rank and directed one of the drivers to take him to the hospital.

'Kids ward, I want. Nearest entrance and as quick as you like.'

The man eased the car into gear and slid forward into the afternoon traffic. 'One of your own, is it?'

'Yea. A car accident this morning . . .'

'Sorry to hear it. How bad is he?'

'It's she. Bad enough and only two and a half.'

'Poor little soul. I remember when mine was that age. You needed eyes in the back of your head. Can't watch them all the time, can you?'

'Should be able to. That's what mothers are for isn't it?'

'You're living in the past, aren't you?'

'She was driving. It was her fucking responsibility.'

'Is she hurt as well?'

'Don't know yet. Don't care much either.'

The driver raised one eyebrow, but said nothing. When Mark reached the Children's ward he discovered that it was locked. He had to ring a bell and wait until a nurse came and opened it to him in a friendly enough way but standing firmly in the doorway while she questioned him about his reasons for being there.

'Abi is comfortable,' she said, 'but her parents are the only people allowed to visit today.'

'Well, can I speak to Mrs Matthews then? My wife's got the twin sister at home and she wants to know what's happening.'

'Abi's twin?' She opened the door and ushered him into a corridor hung with bright mobiles and pictures of wild animals. To one side was the theatre trolley, cleverly disguised as Thomas the Tank Engine in an effort to make hospital life less frightening for the small children unfortunate enough to be here.

'What name did you say?'

'Mark Wyburn.'

'Wait in here and I'll make enquiries.' The room was filled with expensive toys and Mark wondered if Charlie and Lewis would have had the courage to play with them if ever they'd needed to come here.

The nurse was returning. He could just make out the sound of her footsteps approaching along the corridor, so he sat down and tried to look as if this was an everyday occurrence for him.

'One of the parents will pop out and see you when they can,' she said. 'But it could be some time yet.'

'Any chance of a cup of tea?' he said.

144

'There's a machine in Casualty.'

'Can't you make me one? I've had nothing since 7 o'clock this morning.' He gave his most winning smile and winked wickedly in her direction.

'You'll get me into trouble,' she said but crossed the corridor to the kitchen where she put the kettle on and popped two slices of bread into the stainless steel toaster. When it was ready he ate as slowly as he could, but even delaying her with pointless chatter filled only a few minutes. Then he was back in the playroom where dolls stared drunkenly towards him and toy cars piled up in a realistic impression of a road accident. He put his hand in his pocket for a cigarette and then thought better of it. It would never be allowed amongst babies and young children. In the distance a nurse laughed and somewhere closer a baby wailed. Mark wondered what they were doing to it, to cause such distress. And where was Abi? Was she really comfortable or was that just a hospital expression? He stepped out into the long corridor. Already he knew that he wouldn't be in Keswick in time for the five o'clock bus. Roger would wonder where he was and offer his chocolate cake to some other hungry passenger.

'Nurse,' he called. 'Are you there?'

A little boy appeared from a side-ward, his thin legs were supported by callipers and a leather helmet was strapped on to his head. He looked back into the room and laughed and a nurse pretended to chase after him.

'Excuse me,' Mark said.

'Oh hello. Can I help you?'

'Can you tell me where Abi Matthews is?'

'Second room on the right,' she rushed away as the boy swayed to one side. Mark hurried on down the corridor. On one wall a public telephone hung, black and inviting. He lifted the receiver and dialled Roger's mobile number.

'Roger Keogh.'

'Roger, its Mark. Have you had a good day?' . . . . 'I'll not be on the bus at Keswick. I'm at the hospital.' . . . . . 'One of the little uns has had an accident . . .' 'Don't know yet . . .' 'Aye, bad timing, the new job starting on Monday . . .' 'Can you ring them for me if I'm not back?' . . . 'Great. See you mate.'

He turned towards the door and the curtained window that hid Abi and her parents from him. There was no sound from inside - neither calm voices nor painful cries; nothing to give a clue as to what was happening. Without a knock or hesitation of any kind Mark pushed the door and it opened. Abi lay in a high cot and appeared to be sleeping. One little arm was spread out to the side, strapped to a splint to hold it straight so that the blood transfusion could do its work. Mr Matthews sat on a chair with his back to the door but Helen was at the far side looking straight towards him.

'Mark!' Her eyes widened but her head remained still, supported by the surgical collar.

Mr Matthews turned and stood up. 'Is there something wrong with Camilla?'

'No, she's fine.'

'Why have you come here then?'

'That's the thanks I get, is it? Donna wants to know how Abi really is - not just "as comfortable as can be expected" and she wants Mrs Matthews to phone her - about what to do for Camilla and all that. And whether to keep her at our house all night . . .'

'Your house?' Helen's voice was low.

'Where'd you think she is? There wasn't a key for yours, was there?'

'We're not allowed the mobile in here,' Mr Matthews said.

'There's a call-box in the corridor.'

Mr Matthews brought small change from his pocket. 'Show her where it is, Mark, will you?'

146

'I'll find it.'

Mark held the door wide. 'After you,' he said, but when they were safely out of ear-shot he grinned and said 'this is my chance to tell him, isn't it?'

'You pig. At a time like this.'

'Have to grab the main chance,' he said, 'so how much to keep quiet? Or shall I drop a word in?'

'I've nothing here. Tomorrow . . .'

Back in the small ward they explained that there'd been no reply from Donna - too busy with the children probably. A different nurse came in to check on Abi and make sure that the blood was flowing freely. 'B negative, that's an unusual one,' she said.

'Same as me,' Mark said and Helen gave him a startled glance, but Mr Matthews did not appear to notice.

Mark reached through the rails of the cot and ran his finger down Abi's arm and into the palm of her hand. Her fingers closed round his and for a few seconds they were locked together. Helen began to cry and Mr Matthews said 'You'd better go now Mark. It's been an upsetting day for all of us. We'll ring Donna later. It might be best if she can keep Camilla there for the night.'

'No.' The two men stared as Helen rose to her feet. 'No,' she said. 'Camilla should be in her own bed. There's special things she needs . . .'

'I'll give Mark our key then and if *he* can see to the boys, Donna might take Camilla to the flat. It's good of you both. I'll make it worth your while,' he said.

Helen knew instinctively that Mark would go to the flat first. He would go in to the bedroom and rifle through all her things until he found the bank statements, hidden at the very back of the jumper drawer. He would see the rumpled pillows on the bed that she'd left unmade in her hurry to get away from the hotel. And he would notice the creased sheets and Andrew's

147

bible on the bedside cabinet. She couldn't bear the thought of his prying eyes and probing fingers.

'No,' she said again. 'Donna has enough to do. Tell her I'll come home later and get Camilla.'

'But they're keeping you in . . .'

'I'm alright. You can stay here with Abi. I'll see to Camilla. They both need us now.'

Chapter Twenty - Eight.

Kevin thought of the money he'd saved to buy a house and wondered whether to spend it on a car instead. The house was his dream, but a car meant freedom and pleasure and Saturday nights in town with people his own age instead of coming to his room when even the flat across the stable yard would be empty. He'd heard that Abi was out of danger now, but Mr and Mrs Matthews were sure to stay with her until she was better and Camilla was in Donna's house with the two boys where everything felt right, like a real home ought to feel. Just one mother all the time who would scold you when she had to but love you just the same.

His own room was shadowy but not dark enough yet to switch on the light. He crossed to his CD player near the window and out of habit glanced over to the flat. Suddenly he stiffened. A figure moved in the subdued light of a table lamp. Not tall enough for Mr Matthews and too straight for Mrs Matthews, who was supple and attractive and had a habit of tossing her head so that her fine hair flew out like a halo. As he watched, another figure crossed the yard and peeped in at the lighted window, then knocked at the door with a bang that could be heard quite clearly in Kevin's quiet room.

If he'd spent some of his money on a mobile phone he could have sent for the police or he could have rung the hospital and told Mr Matthews what was happening. Instead he kept quite still and watched the man barge his way in, as soon as the door was unlocked and a moment later reappear in full view of the living room window.

When the two figures sat down opposite each other, it occurred to Kevin that this was not the way he would have expected a burglar to behave. He was risking a lot, sitting there with the light on even though it was unlikely anybody would walk into the yard or go across to the flat. Suddenly it wasn't enough to close his curtains and get on with his own life. He needed some excitement to liven the lonely evening. Sneaking across the yard in the shadow of the buildings would provide it and crouching below the window would probably let him hear what was being said.

Outside the new moon showed palely against the darkening sky and Kevin remembered how his mother had always made a wish when she'd seen it. He wondered if it had been the wrong time for wishing when Mark walked away and left her or had she seen the new moon through glass and brought on the bad luck that she talked about so often? Now he stared at the sky and wished that his own life would open up so that he could have something more exciting than serving other people in this staid lake-district hotel.

Down here the sound of voices escaped from the old sash windows of the flat. A man's voice dominated the conversation, but the words were unclear. Kevin crept round the edge of the yard keeping carefully within the shadows. If the door opened he would be seen then he could lose his job for spying on the manager's home. He would have wasted his apprenticeship and given away his good reputation. He would have no possibility of buying either a home or a car. But it would all be worth it for the excitement of these few precious minutes.

Now he was within inches of the window, flattening himself against the wall and listening to the voices that became clearer as he approached. The man's voice was bullying and demanding and also strangely familiar. The other voice was softer and seemed to be appealing, although the words were still not distinct. Kevin dropped below the white-painted window-sill keeping his head low until he was certain that the conversation was continuing and he hadn't been noticed.

Gradually he allowed his head to rise until it was high enough for him to see inside the room. Mrs Matthews was

150

sitting directly opposite. She was wearing a surgical collar that kept her chin high and her head still. Kevin strained to hear what she was saying but could only pick out odd words. However her body language was clear enough. Her visitor was not welcome and she couldn't make him leave.

The man's voice *did* penetrate the window. He wanted money and he wanted it now. There was no sign of a parcel or goods of any kind that he was offering in exchange. It sounded like blackmail. And it was nasty.

Suddenly the man rose to his feet and crossed to the mantelpiece, but still his face was in shadow. He picked up a white china figure and with his arm stretched out in front of him he moved the ornament up and down then he let it fall, but caught it again with his other hand causing Mrs Matthews to draw in her breath with a quick gasping sound.

'Am I getting it, then?' the man said and something in his manner became familiar. Kevin remembered a dark night, a figure in the shadows and the pain of a cigarette burn.

I can't understand our Mark missing his bus back to Durham - not with the new job starting on Monday and after all this long time out of work. But once he heard about the accident there was no stopping him. He just had *to go to the hospital and find out about little Abi. And he's over at the flat now seeing if Mrs Matthews is alright. Mark has a real kind side to him, but it'll mean him going back by train and it takes forever on Sundays* and *costs a fortune that we haven't got.*

Chapter Twenty-Nine.

The house was in darkness. It stood in a row of identical properties lit only by a lamp at the corner, where the narrow road joined the major one into the centre of town.

Mark turned the key gingerly in the lock, but as the door opened, the staircase flooded with light and Roger appeared on the landing in the sort of pyjamas Mark hadn't worn since he was a boy.

'That *is* you, isn't it Mark?'

'I was trying not to wake you.'

'It's alright. I was keeping an ear open for you. Glad you've made it. I'll get you a coffee . . .'

'No thanks, mate. I'd better get my head down for a couple of hours. I've had to fucking hitch and believe me, it wasn't easy.'

'Good night then and good luck.'

When the alarm sounded a few hours later, Mark forced himself to get out of bed. He would have liked a shower, but it would mean missing breakfast and it was a long time since he'd had anything to eat. He simply splashed his face with cold water, decided that yesterday's shave would last him, and went downstairs to make strong coffee and eat as many cornflakes as he could pack into the ample green bowl. He was sorry to leave Roger without milk. The man had been fantastic, helping a stranger the way he'd done, but Mark would repay him as soon as he was earning again. Without this place to stay and with no car, the job would have been impossible.

He started to walk towards the factory, knowing that it had been a very lucky day for him when he met up with Roger Keogh. As he got nearer, he was overtaken by cars of every size and shape, usually with only the driver in them. A few men straggled through the gates and trudged up the long road to the buildings where they would be working for the next twelve hours. One or two greetings rang out, but Mark was simply accepted as one of the workforce and the feeling gave him confidence and he imagined the days when he would set out from his own home, knowing that Donna was there and would be waiting for him when he got back at the end of the shift.

* * * * *

The machine was enormous and dark. The noise was constant, accentuated by an extra resounding bang that was repeated every few minutes. The window was too high, even for the tall black man to see through as he lifted and turned and heaved car parts off the machine and out to the side of the small workshop.

'This is Hughie,' the supervisor was saying, 'he'll show you the ropes. You'll soon get into the way of it and he'll be thankful you've started. Isn't that right, Hughie?' Without waiting for a reply the man made to go and Mark pulled himself together.

'Here, this isn't what I was taken on to do.'

The man paused. 'No?'

'No. I'm here to work with the new robots. That girl . . . Fiona . . . she explained it all to us. We're going to be the first ones to operate them.'

'Hear that, Hughie? Enough to make your sides split, isn't it?'

'Told me the same thing, boss. And that's over two years ago now.'

'But you can't do this. My contract's to work with robots.'

'Is that right? Why d'you think they chose the three biggest men then?' He disappeared, chuckling to himself as he went. Mark stood in the doorway, and knew that he couldn't do it. Not even for Donna's sake, could he exist in that terrible

153

space. And he'd never seen any man with such physique.

'You'll get used to it, you know. At least it pays the mortgage and buys the bairns new shoes,' the man said.

Mark snorted as Hughie went on. 'I'm doing a college course as well. I'll get out of this if it kills me. But it takes time.'

'What sort of course?'

'Computers.'

'Computers?' Mark looked at Hughie with new respect. Perhaps the man was human after all. 'Right, give me the low-down on this lot then.'

* * * * *

The oil spluttered and rose dangerously near to the top of the pan, as Roger lowered the basket of raw chips into it. Some day he would treat himself to a deep-fat fryer that was safer and cleaner but in the meantime, he made the best chips in town and he was always careful to stay near while he was cooking them. Besides, if he stood a fat-fryer on his work top, there'd be no room for anything else.

He slotted the grill-pan into place. A man like Mark would like his steak rare and he'd be here at any minute now. Roger sliced an onion into thin rings and reached for a bottle of red wine, just as he heard the knock on the front door.

Mark had his key to the house and Roger felt inclined to ignore the noise rather than spoil the meal. However as he hesitated, the knocks became frantic. He lifted the pan off the gas and pulled the steak away from the heat, then walked along the narrow passage to the front door. The shadow of a man's head showed through the obscure glass and Roger realised it was Mark.

'Have you forgotten your key?' He began as he unlocked the door, then he reached forward as Mark stumbled and almost fell into the house.

'No,' his voice was faint. 'Couldn't do it, Roger. I'm

done.'

'You're just tired. Hitching back here last night and hardly any sleep . . .'

'No. It's too hard.' Mark let his weight fall against Roger and was thankful for the man's support as he grabbed at the door frame to steady himself.

'You'll feel better when you've eaten. I'll put it on a tray and bring it through here.'

'I can't.' Mark shook his head and dropped into the nearest chair. Roger had an awful feeling he was going to cry so he disappeared towards the kitchen and came back with two glasses of wine then sat opposite Mark on the brown leather couch. After a few minutes, Mark said 'It's not what they promised. They only wanted strongmen. What am I going to do, Roger?'

'Eat first, a good night's sleep and try another day.'

'I can't go back.'

'What about Donna? You can't let her down without a try, can you?'

I was sure Mark would've rung tonight. I've been keeping near this phone since half past six and I even tried 1471 after I'd been upstairs with the boys. But there's nothing. I've got Roger's number, but I don't like to ring him. You never know where people were going to be when it's a mobile. It might be awkward. I'm just frightened Mark had an accident last night. I don't like him hitching lifts like a bit of a kid, although he should be alright knowing the roads like he does.

From his chair near the window, Roger caught a first glimpse of Mark. He'd been relieved to hear the front door close at 5.30 that morning. The man had guts, to go back after the disappointment of the previous day and hopefully he'd come to terms with the work, even if it was only until he got his licence

155

back and could apply for driving jobs again. However, when Roger saw him trudging home again he knew that it was no good. Although Mark was in better shape than the previous night, his whole attitude spoke of despair and Roger went to open the door and welcome him back.

'I've given it my best shot, but it's no good. I can't do it,' Mark said and was on his way upstairs. 'Hughie says a lot of the lads never turn up again after the first day.'

'They'll lose their benefit then.'

'Aye, that's the fucking catch, isn't it?' He disappeared into the bathroom and Roger listened as the shower began to run at full force, but there was no sound of the singing that had amused him so much since Mark had come to the house. He went to his desk and got out writing paper and envelopes, then he sat down and composed a letter for Mark to copy and send to the firm, stating that they had broken their side of the contract and he would leave at the end of the first week. Hopefully, that way he *would* be able to claim benefit again and look for another job without prejudice. But of course, Mark would have to talk to Donna and that was going to be the hardest part of it all.

I can't believe it. Not that I blame Mark. They should never have said anything about those robots. Letting them think it was something special like that. And I'm not saying he should've stayed either, but I got the lists of houses, this morning. Renee phoned round the agents and asked for them. And there's one I really like and I was going to go over there and have a look. His mam said she'd keep the boys and she said to be sure and get one with an extra bedroom, in case she decides to come and live with us. Well at least that won't happen now.

156

Chapter Thirty.

Helen thought of all the Saturdays she'd spent at the Ascot hotel. The long days in the flat when she'd been so lonely that she'd allowed Mark Wyburn to visit her even though she knew he would walk over to the main building afterwards, collect Donna and take her back to their cottage in the village. Then there was the Saturday when Helen had told him she was pregnant and he'd denied that the child was his. On the same day she'd delighted Andrew with the news of the approaching birth.

How upset she'd been a few Saturdays later when she'd seen Mark proudly wheeling Donna's new baby round the hotel gardens and how incredible it seemed that it had been Mark who'd driven her back from the post office the day when the labour pains had caught her unawares. Even more incredible was the fact that he should now be blackmailing her on as many Saturdays as he could find her.

Even the accident had been on a Saturday. Now, exactly one week later Abi was about to be discharged from hospital. But there would be no car-rides to divert them for several Saturdays to come. Helen doubted if she'd have had the nerve to drive, even if the car had not been pronounced a write-off by the insurance company. It seemed that Saturdays, like all other days, would be stay-at-home ones for the time being.

When Andrew carried Abi into the flat at lunchtime the child was strangely withdrawn and refused all Helen's attempts to cuddle her. Instead, she crossed to Camilla's chair and stood close beside her as if their separation had been too much to bear. Andrew made an effort to stay cheerful and ate one of the sausages that were usually Abi's favourites, then on the pretext of catching up on work he hurried away. As he left the house Mrs Kell walked across the yard carrying a gift bag in each hand.

'I'm glad I've caught you,' she said. 'These are for Abi and Camilla. My husband will never forgive himself for what happened . . .'

'But it wasn't his fault. The police say he was travelling slowly . . .'

'He should have been able to avoid it after all the years he's been driving. Thousands of miles a year, he's done but of course we've both got a lot on our minds just now.' She took a deep breath and with an obvious effort managed to control her voice. 'Anyway, these are baby dolls for them. They deserve it after what they've been through.'

'It's very kind,' Andrew began, but she waved it aside. 'We're going home now. Fortunately the car's drivable and he feels well enough to cope. But we'll be back to see you again later in the year.'

'We'll look forward to it. Take care, both of you.'

The dolls closed their eyes and cried real tears. Helen was touched by the kindness of this elderly couple who had so much sadness in their own lives but the thought of what might have happened filled her with horror and she wondered how they could ever forgive her.

I decide to pop over to the flat just before tea-time. I've got a nice bunch of stocks for Mrs Matthews and picture books for the girls. They're a bit old for them really, but it's all Mrs Monaghan had.

Mrs Matthews is ever so grateful, and she has such lovely manners. 'You'll be getting Mark off for his bus,' she says, 'don't let us keep you.'

But I say 'No. The job wasn't what he expected.'

'Will he be looking for something else over there?' she says.

'No,' I say. 'He's had enough. He wants to be at home again. We'll manage somehow till he gets his licence back

again.'

I don't know how she can think about other people at a time like this.

For the second time in his life Mark felt humiliated. Being disqualified from driving had been a blow that could happen to anybody who was unlucky enough to be stopped by the police at just the wrong moment. But failing at his job was another thing and one that had knocked his confidence completely. He'd never imagined that such a thing could happen to him. Roger had helped him to extricate himself from the awkward situation. Donna had been understanding and his mother had been protective, but Mark was angry with a deep, dark anger that burnt away at him as he tried to reconcile himself to the boredom of village life and the thinly veiled contempt that he could see in other people's eyes.

He'd always thought of himself as a hard man who could cope with anything life threw at him. Now he knew that he was just as vulnerable as everybody else.

In the space of a week he'd worked with Hughie, who was bigger and stronger and more powerful than any man he'd ever known. And he'd lived with Roger, who was generous and kind, but so domesticated that it had baffled Mark. He'd even wished there was a lock on his bedroom door, although to be fair the man had never come on to him. Yet he was strangely unnerved by Roger's suggestion of coming to the Ascot some Saturday instead of staying in the bus and going all the way to Kendal. Mark had insisted on paying rent out of the wage he got for the one week's work and that should have been the end of it. A business deal, nothing more nor less.

Yet now, a month later, Roger was coming, and not just for a day. He'd actually booked into the Ascot for a whole week. Donna had taken the call last night while Mark was walking the countryside in an effort to pass the time and use up some of his

159

surplus energy. Now he wished he'd been here to put the man off. He could have made up some reason on the spur of the moment - said they were going away that week or he was doing some casual work. As it was he'd be expected to entertain the man and he'd get little support from Donna because she'd be working overtime, thankful that the hotel was busy and she had a chance to earn extra money

At least she'd prepared some lunch for them all and she'd be home in time to serve it. Roger would find their cottage cluttered after the calm of his own house and Mark wondered why that mattered to him. However, when Roger finally arrived with remarkably little luggage for a week's stay, he was charming to Donna and complimentary about their home.

'You're a lucky man, Mark. I can see why you said you had the best wife in the Lake District . . .'

Donna blushed and found it hard to believe that Mark even felt that, never mind put it into words.

'You must be glad to be home in spite of the disappointment of the job. Rotten trick that was. Put it down to experience, though.' He reached for the salad cream and poured it liberally over his plate, smiling at the boys who watched his every move.

'Aye, that's how I am looking at it.' Mark said. 'Nothing round here though. They take students on for the summer jobs. Free board and pay them peanuts.'

'Hard luck. How much longer till you get the licence back?'

'March next year. Seems like a life-time.'

'It must do, but it'll soon come round and then you'll be alright again. And I can see Donna's a big support,' he said.

'We don't starve,' Mark said and Donna shook her head and wondered if he had any idea how difficult it sometimes was to provide the amount of food he took so much for granted. When the meal was over Mark and the boys offered to take

160

Roger over to the hotel. 'Have you got your key? Mark said.

'Yes. It's room 83.'

'83? That's the Grooms' Cottages.' There'd be no spying on Helen this week or even just watching his daughters play. 'Come on boys, let's show Roger the way.' Mark hoisted Lewis on to his shoulder, then he picked Roger's bag up with his other hand. 'You travel light. I'll say that for you.'

'Years of practice. I've got it off to a fine art by now.' The little procession set off along the drive with Charlie always a few steps ahead. Roger looked at Lewis, whose face was so close to Mark's. 'You couldn't deny he was yours, could you?' He laughed, then he went on more soberly. 'You never did tell me about that accident. Did he get over it alright?'

'Oh, I was too busy trying to sort the job out.' Mark quickly looked away, afraid that Roger would notice something was wrong. Then to change the subject, he pointed ahead. 'That's the new pool. If you like swimming you'll be alright there.'

'I might very well do that. What's the quietest time?'

'It never gets very busy. But watch out for the fella with the one leg.'

'Who?'

'He's a guest. Comes four or fives times a year. He's just arrived again this morning. You'll likely see him - he usually has 82, next to yours.'

'You seem to be well informed.' Roger frowned and thought how little he knew this man, yet he'd invited him into his home and might have had him there yet if the job had been what Mark expected.

'I keep my eyes open. And Donna's working among the guests all the time. She's very popular and she picks up a good few tips, as well . . .'

'I'm sure she does. So what's the matter with this poor chap then?'

161

'Had a leg off, that's all I know and when he goes swimming he leaves the false one in the changing rooms. He crawls in,' Mark shuddered and his face clouded over. 'Shouldn't be allowed, that's what I say.'

'Live and let live.'

'Aye well, you must have a longer fuse than me.'

Roger looked round with interest as they entered the building known as the Grooms' Cottages. Even in the middle of the day it was gloomy and he quickly brought out the key he'd been given at reception while Mark fingered its replica safely lying in his own pocket.

As if on cue the door of number 82 opened and Paul Hutchinson came into the narrow passage. 'You here again, Wyburn?' he said.

'Looks like it, doesn't it?' Before Paul could answer Roger reappeared and Mark introduced him with mock civility.

'Roger Keogh, Paul Hutchinson. Paul Hutchinson, Roger Keogh,' he said and bowed his head respectfully.

'Right, well I hope you're quieter than some I could mention.' Paul said and went back into his own room.

'Charmer,' Roger mouthed and Charlie giggled until his father flicked his hand hard against the child's head making him cry out in pain. Then he was quiet. Roger hated violence of any kind, but especially against a child.

'Thank you for lunch,' he said, trying to cover his disapproval. 'We certainly made it last, didn't we? Now don't put yourselves out over me. The evening meal's at seven and there's some entertainment afterwards. Tomorrow we're visiting Sizergh Castle to see the famous limestone rock garden, so you enjoy the weekend with your family and I'll catch up with you later.' With that he went into his room and began to unpack.

Mark seethed at the easy dismissal and as an act of defiance he banged the flat of his hand hard on to Paul's door before striding out of the building with Charlie running to keep

162

up. Paul stepped back into the corridor and watched the outside door close behind them then he went back to drink the black coffee he'd just made and listen to the rumble of bath water in the pipes that was soon loud enough to drown the sound of Handel's Water Music on his radio. At least, he thought this Roger Keogh bathed in the daytime so he was unlikely to do it again in the early hours of the morning. That was something to be thankful for.

* * * * *

The evening meal proved to be excellent. Kevin was efficient and good humoured and Roger decided the boy was destined for bigger and better hotels than this one.

The company was pleasant and the conversation stimulating at the large round table that held eight guests. It was disappointing, therefore, to find that the entertainment afterwards was nothing more than paper-and-pencil games and a "getting to know you" session. As soon as he reasonably could Roger made his escape, slipping away through empty lounges in the direction of the main door and the path back to his own room. However, when he reached Reception he discovered that he was not the only one who was bored by the evening. Paul Hutchinson was sitting at the table nearest the window with a glass of whisky in front of him.

'Is that not your scene either?' Roger asked, rather than walking past without speaking.

'Waste of time.' Paul said.

Roger nodded. 'Mind if I join you for a few minutes?'

'It's a free country.'

Roger took that as permission and sat down opposite him while Paul drained the last drops of his drink. 'New to the lakes, are you?' Paul asked.

'New to this hotel, but I know the area well. I come across every Saturday when there's a direct bus.'

163

'Do you now? Are you a walker?'

'Short walks. I'm tied to bus times, you know.'

'I was a walker . . . before this.' Paul tapped his hand against the artificial leg and Roger made a sympathetic face and wondered whether he was meant to ask about it.

'Was it an accident? He enquired, keeping his voice level.

'No. It was not.'

'Sorry, none of my business.'

'You're right it isn't, but if you must know I had a health problem and had to take special care of myself . . . and still this happened.'

Roger shook his head. 'Unbelievable,' he said.

'Never mind, I can still swim. Reckon to do a thousand lengths in the two weeks I'm here. That friend of yours doesn't approve of course, but then he has no right to be in the pool. He's not a guest.'

'I suppose not.'

'You want to watch your step with that one. Nasty piece of work, he is . . . Now I'm going to my room. Goodnight to you.'

'I'll walk across with you.'

'As you like.' Paul got to his feet and walked outside. He'd have preferred to be alone but he could hardly be downright rude to the man.

Daylight was already fading and there was a chill in the air that spoke of autumn. Roger found it hard to make small talk as Paul trod the familiar path to the annexe, so he simply walked beside him until they reached their own rooms. 'See you tomorrow,' he said.

'Probably. I expect you'll not be running the bath water in the early hours of the morning.'

'What?'

'Wyburn does whenever he's here. Don't know what you see in the man.' He closed his door with a thud and Roger was

164

left to wonder what his words could possibly mean.

Next morning when Roger woke the annexe was very quiet, the stable yard deserted and the flat opposite showed no sign of life but the sun was shining and it promised to be a fine day. He missed the space of his own bedroom. This one was narrow and the louvered pine doors loomed over him, so he quickly got out of bed and pulled them wide open. The familiar sight of soap and sponge and a yellow towel folded ready at one end were more acceptable to him than the slatted wood that concealed them. He was tempted to run the taps and wallow in a deep luxurious bath, but Paul's warning from the night before stopped him, even though 6.45 could hardly be classed as the early hours.

The veiled comments that Paul had made hinted at a different side to Mark. Roger had only ever seen him as a family man, doing the best he could for his wife and children. Now it seemed he was a more complex character and Roger wondered if he had been wise to try to be his friend. But the thought was depressing and he quickly began to dress and move about. Action was what was needed now. He must get out of this room and walk round the grounds until he found another human being to speak to. He opened a drawer to look for clean socks but instead found swimming trunks folded neatly beside a bright towel. Some earlier guest must be missing those, but he rolled the two together and pushed his feet into open sandals then he left the room as quietly as he could.

The gardens were deserted. The umbrellas that usually shaded the tables were still bright poles in the morning sunshine. The day already had enough warmth to dry the well-cut lawns. In the hotel guests were beginning to open their curtains and look out at the hills and the estuary and catch sight of the gulls that screeched their lonely cry. But the main door was still locked.

Roger made his way along the footpath and under the old

165

tree until he came to the wicket gate then instead of turning towards the Halt he went through the village and found the first sign of life at the post office where Mrs Monaghan was organising boys to deliver the Sunday papers to people who had not yet started the day.

'Morning,' she called. 'It's going to be a lovely day.'

'Morning,' he called back and began to believe that it would be. He quickened his stride and walked on, through the main gate, back into the hotel grounds and towards the new swimming pool. It was a long time since he'd been swimming so it would be good to have the place to himself for a while. However as soon as he walked into the changing room he knew that Paul Hutchinson had beaten him to it. An artificial leg leaned against the lockers, discreetly waiting to be reclaimed when its owner collected the rest of his belongings.

Roger stood still and stared at it, trying to imagine what life must be like for somebody who depended on it for every step he took. It would need not only determination and courage but physical strength as well.

When he stood by the pool a few minutes later he could see Paul's head and shoulders moving up and down as he cut through the water with incredible speed. When he reached the deep end he turned and headed back towards the point where Roger waited.

'I'm coming out,' he called. 'If you're squeamish, look away. Mark Wyburn does. Are you a man or a mouse, that's the question?'

'Man. Most definitely man.'

'Not like your friend then. He's mouse, certainly.' With that Paul heaved himself up the steps.

'You do well.' Roger said.

'Leave it alone. I'm a freak,' said Paul moving the stump of his leg. 'I know it and you know it and Wyburn certainly knows it. He plays on weakness, low-down skunk that he is.'

166

'I think you're exaggerating . . .'

'I know what I know and Mrs Matthews would say the same if she wasn't afraid of her husband finding out.' He crawled across the tiled floor in the direction of the changing room but paused before he reached it. 'You can always ask the young waiter, if you need proof. Kevin's the name. Ask young Kevin.'

Roger had lost the desire to swim now, but rather than speak to Paul again he walked halfway along the side of the pool then slid slowly into the water. After so many years away he allowed himself to test it gradually.

Chapter Thirty-One.

Sizergh Castle was fascinating, a good start to the week's activities. Roger had half-hoped that Paul might be with them but as it was Roger was the only single person there and nobody invited him to join them as they wandered from room to room admiring the fine Elizabethan furniture and marvelling at the splendour of the 14th century building that had belonged to the same family for all those years. One generation had followed another, never a break, never an ending. He sighed. His own family was petering out and so was Paul Hutchinson's, but Mark Wyburn's was flourishing. Two sons to carry on the family name, both inheriting their father's looks and strength but if Paul's hints were to be believed they could have inherited less pleasant streaks as well.

Roger was used to being alone so apart from a smile or an occasional word with anybody who happened to be standing next to him he simply accepted the situation. Nevertheless he was quite relieved when it was time to return to the coach and he was one of the first to be on it. He laid his head back and closed his eyes. It had been a long day but now that he was quiet he thought about the conversation he'd had with Paul that morning. He wondered what to make of its disturbing undercurrents and thought he might have been wiser to stay right away from the Ascot hotel, instead of breaking the habit of a life-time to book a week's holiday there.

He'd intended to invite Mark and Donna over for a meal and to stay on for the entertainment that was designed for young families like theirs. Now he wondered whether to postpone the meeting for a day or two. No doubt they would be offended by his non-appearance but it would give him time to do some checking up first. On the other hand it might be more interesting to watch Kevin's reaction when he was obliged to serve a meal

168

to Mark Wyburn. So Roger waited until he was out of the coach and back in his own room before picking up his mobile phone and ringing Mark's number.

I was thankful when we got the phone call from Roger. Mark's been in a right mood since Saturday. Said he wished he'd never met him in the first place. Of course, if he hadn't he couldn't have had the job over there, but then he'd never have failed at it either so I suppose it might have been better. He's taken badly to things lately, first the licence, then the job. Anyway he's tickled to death about us going over to the Ascot tonight. I'm not so sure myself. It might be a bit embarrassing. I don't know what Mr Matthews'll say about one of his domestics sitting down with all the guests.

'Lovely to see you again, Donna. How are you, Mark?' Roger welcomed them at the front door, noting how they'd dressed up for the evening. Mark's white shirt strained at the collar, the loose button at the top covered by an extra large knot in his navy-blue tie. Donna wore black. A large glass brooch was pinned to the lapel of her jacket. Her sandals were the ones she'd bought before Lewis was born. She'd kept them for special occasions and there'd been very few of those.

'You haven't brought the boys?' Roger said.

'No. They're with my mother,' Mark said.

'We wouldn't inflict them on *you*,' Donna put in. 'Not at a special meal like this.'

'It's a family hotel. Children are welcome.'

'I'd never have had a minute's peace, especially if Kevin was serving . . .'

'Why's that then?'

'He used to spend a lot of time at our house. He's like a big brother to them.'

'Does he not come now?'

169

'Not very often. Not since Mark was there so much at any rate.'

'There's enough of us in the house as it is. No room for extras.' Mark growled.

'Right. Well let's go through then,' Roger said. 'They're big tables - of course you'll know that Donna. I kept five places for us, thinking the boys were coming as well.' He led the way to the table beside the window, knowing that it was one of Kevin's. Then he carefully positioned them with their backs to the room. He wanted to see Kevin's reaction when he walked round the table and faced them for the first time.

Three other people were already at the table laughing and talking about the day's outing. They merely nodded and smiled at the newcomers, then continued the conversation where they'd left off. At the last minute Paul came in, hesitating in the doorway, scanning the room for an empty place. The tables closest to him were taken and were already being served. The room buzzed with noise and it was a few minutes before he spotted the empty seats near the window. He grunted to himself. One of his pet hates was to walk right across the room between busy tables. There was always somebody who hadn't pulled his chair far enough in and Paul would have to ask him to do it or else hold on to it as he passed. Either way he attracted attention so by the time he reached Roger's table he was very disgruntled and dropped on to the nearest chair without taking notice of the people already there.

'Evening Paul,' Roger said and he looked up.

'Evening,' he began. 'Wyburn! What the hell's he doing here?'

'I have as much right as you,' Mark said. 'I've been invited.'

'Have you? Well I'm not sitting next to you and that's a fact.'

He struggled to his feet. Donna leaned forward to look

170

past both Roger and Mark. 'There's an empty chair next to me, Paul. You come and sit here,' she said.

'"You come and sit here," ' Mark mimicked her. 'You'd think there was something going on between you two.'

The other people at the table stopped talking and stared uneasily as Paul moved round and took his place next to Donna.

'That's right,' she said. 'You'll be alright there.'

'Blasted Mother Theresa.' Mark muttered, but caught a warning look from Roger and turned his attention to the menu. 'I'll have the soup,' he said. 'Shouldn't think there's much in prawn cocktails.'

The others relaxed and began to talk about the excursion to Kirby Lonsdale next day. At the same time Kevin threaded his way across the room. One of the younger waiters had warned him there was something going on at his table near the window and he'd quickly changed his order of working and gone to serve that one next.

'Evening everybody,' he smiled encouragingly and walked round the table so that he had his back to the light, 'Have you all had a nice . . . '

'Hallo love,' Donna said. 'You wouldn't expect us tonight.'

But Kevin's eyes were on Mark. Never in his worst nightmare had he imagined Mark Wyburn sitting at a table in the Ascot hotel for all the world like one of the ordinary guests. But he wasn't ordinary. He was a monster. For a moment Kevin was a little boy again, watching Mark parading round the kitchen in the silk dressing gown. Then seeing the cord from the same dressing gown round his mother's neck as she swung from the banisters after Mark had left her. He shivered and put his hand to his face where there was still a faint burn mark near the right eye.

Roger watched closely as Kevin made a great effort and managed to pull himself together.

'Are you ready to order now?' he asked.

'Too right we are,' Mark said. 'I'll have the soup and make sure it's hot.'

I can't stay here, not if he's going to hit me. He's never done it before, but I should have been more careful. It was stupid taking Paul Hutchinson's side at the table like that. I suppose it showed Mark up in public and he can't stand that.

But I didn't deserve this. Still it's not as if it's a black eye or anything. Nobody can see your ribs, so I'll be able to go about as usual. I'd better not ring our Renee. I know what she'd say.

It was a long time since Roger had allowed himself the luxury of a deep bath. At home, he used the shower, always conscious of the water meter ticking away under the kitchen sink, producing another bill to be paid at the end of every quarter. Now he ran the taps, causing the noisy rumble in the pipes that always resulted in Paul's radio being turned high in protest. He laughed to himself. Even that proved that he had a neighbour and was better than the silence he was used to in his own home. He switched on the light above the bath and the low reading lamp near the bed, then he turned off the main light in its frilly pink shade.

The water relaxed him. He laid back and enjoyed the strange experience of having a bath in his bedroom. When the hotel was first built as a home for some wealthy family, servants must have run up and down the stairs with jugs of hot water to fill hip baths for the people lucky enough to sit in front of blazing fires while they washed away the dirt of the day. But of course, this annexe had been the place where the grooms lived and there would be no baths here. Only the pump in the stable yard for them.

The water pipes finally settled to an uneasy silence and the

172

music was turned back to an acceptable level. Roger relaxed and thought about the difficult events of the evening. The atmosphere over dinner had convinced him beyond any doubt that Kevin was afraid of Mark.

A few minutes later he was sitting up straight and glancing uneasily over his shoulder. Was there somebody in the corridor or had he imagined a slight sound at the door behind him? He grabbed a towel from the shelf above the bath and told himself to keep calm. This was a hotel. There was bound to be noise. He forced himself to sit down but did not lie back in the water again. Instead he picked up the soap, lathered himself quickly and a few minutes later was out and dressed. While the bath water ran away Roger opened the door and glanced into the corridor. It was empty. His imagination had been working overtime.

Chapter Thirty-Two.

It was Wednesday so the excursion would be Grasmere, Keswick and Mirehouse. It would leave at 9.45 and when it returned the guests would be clutching packets of Sarah Nelson Gingerbread and whatever they'd bought from the Cumberland Pencil Museum.

Helen had seen it all before. She wondered how Andrew could stand the monotony of this life but presumably it was easier to organise the programme at the beginning of the season and repeat it at regular intervals rather than plan a new one whenever this holiday appeared on the list.

Outside it was misty. The sort of mist that could turn to steady rain or equally well lift by the middle of the morning and produce a perfect late summer day. Helen opened the front door and stepped outside, holding her hand palm up to check whether it had already started to rain. In the room opposite somebody straightened the net curtain, twitching it into place until it hung in perfect folds across the window. Whoever was in there must be very particular. Often the curtain was caught up for a whole week so that if anybody cared to look they had a clear view across to her flat. She didn't like that and she'd had to ask Donna to alter it more than once lately. Strangely enough it often happened when nobody was booked in so it could only be the fault of the domestics, skimping the work in a room that was rarely needed. She made a note to mention it to Andrew. There'd been some casual staff lately, mostly students who were more eager to earn money than to care about the well-being of the hotel.

Inside the flat, Abi and Camilla played side by side and for once they were peaceful. Helen glanced at the clock. If she worked for an hour it would still only be coffee time then she could bundle the girls into the car and drive them to Bowness

174

where they could feed the swans at the edge of the lake. The car that Andrew had chosen to replace her beautiful silver one was small and cramped and less powerful. She hated it and she hated him for buying it without consulting her, but she knew she was being punished for allowing Abi to be injured and there was nothing she could do about it.

At least she'd got a car. There had been a time when it seemed she wouldn't. It had been the lowest point in her whole life. So when the little Citroen was delivered to her door one morning she had seemed suitably grateful and Andrew had accepted her thanks as his due. However when she drove round the Lakeland roads she had to remind herself that the car lacked the power of the old one. Once or twice she'd forgotten and pulled out at a junction only to realise her mistake and be thankful that she didn't cause another accident.

Now that Mark was at home so much she had become jumpy, keeping the chain on the door and checking who was there before she opened it. She'd even begun to imagine a shadow at the kitchen window although it would have meant that somebody had scaled the high brick wall and risked being seen in the small yard that had no hiding place.

She wanted to be away from the Ascot hotel, somewhere where Mark wouldn't find her and she could relax and breathe easily again. However all her efforts to persuade Andrew to move had come to nothing. This was his world and he was satisfied with it.

A knock at the front door made her jump, but instead of moving towards it she stood quite still in the shady spot between the kitchen and the living room. She hoped that Abi and Camilla were too engrossed to notice it, but it was a vain hope. Both girls looked up at the sound and Abi immediately left her game and crossed to the window. Since Mark had started to demand money from Helen she'd had a blind fitted. It made the room darker and she hated it, but at least it meant that he couldn't spy

175

on her anymore. Now as she watched from the hall she was dismayed to see that Abi knew exactly how to open it. With unerring precision the child reached for the appropriate string and pulled on it. The white slats moved back and Abi waved to the person outside.

'Come away Abi,' Helen said.

'But he's . . .'

'Now, I said.'

Helen went to the door. She'd wanted a spy-hole fitted but Andrew had scorned the idea. This was a hotel. Its whole purpose was to encourage strangers to come and to offer them hospitality. She checked that the chain was in place. Then she turned the key and opened the door just wide enough to peep out.

As Abi had said, it *was* a man; one that Helen had never seen before.

'Good morning,' he said.

'Yes?'

'I believe you're the manager's wife, so you would know the area well.'

'The receptionist'll help you, if you're staying here.'

'Roger Keogh . . . in room 83 just opposite.'

Helen didn't answer.

'There's nobody about so I thought you might be kind enough to give me some directions,' he went on. 'Excuse me for asking but are you always so safety conscious?'

'You can't be too careful.'

'I can assure you I'm perfectly harmless. If you would take the chain off it would make conversation much easier.' Roger smiled and wished that he could get a better view of Mrs Matthews. As it was he could barely see her through the crack in the door and the child had disappeared from the window, obediently closing the blind behind her.

'What do you want to know?'

'A few details about today's excursion.'

176

'They'll tell you on the coach. The driver does a commentary all the way. Have a good day, Mr Keogh.' With that she shut the door and Roger heard the key turn in the lock. He'd wanted proof of Paul Hutchinson's accusations and he'd got it. Mrs Matthews was a very frightened woman.

Mrs Matthews is out early this morning. Since she got that little car she's hardly been off the roads. Of course, it's nowhere near as good as the silver one but she must like it or she wouldn't drive it so much. She's a lucky woman. Just the two children to look after and a husband that gives her everything she wants. I bet he doesn't break her ribs for her. I wish I could remember not to breathe in so hard.

Helen kept the windows closed but opened the sun roof to allow warm air to circulate round the car. Andrew had had two child seats permanently fixed into the back before the car was delivered. It ensured the girls' safety but restricted Helen to family outings only.

As she edged away then waited at the junction to the main road, she was surprised at the amount of traffic that was heading towards Bowness and Windermere. Suddenly she didn't want to be part of the holiday scene, to wander along the shore and let the children feed the swans while the motor boats set off on tours of the lake and the craft shops sold their goods at extortionist prices.

On an impulse she took the turning towards Lancaster while the children sang nursery rhymes to music from a well-worn tape. The further she got, the more she relaxed she became so it seemed right to keep on driving and by the time she was crossing the Pennines the children had sensed her change of mood and fallen asleep in their seats.

Thankfully she turned off the music and drove in a silence that was broken only by the sound of the traffic that passed her on the bleak road. To either side the moors stretched as far as the eye could see. Isolated farmhouses dotted the landscape in picturesque beauty.

As she approached the highest point mist hung over the hills and she needed her headlights to pick out the way ahead. As suddenly as it had come the mist lifted and she was looking at the wide expanse of Bowes Moor stretching away to the east. After the glowering mountains of the Lake District it was a relief to see flat land.

Half an hour later she left the main road and followed country lanes, turning the car first left and then right until the scenery changed and she was driving between tall trees and the view ahead was of forests, dark and dense with rain clouds scudding across the sky.

When a brown sign pointed to Westgarth Castle, she decided to go in, in the hope of finding a visitors' centre where they might eat. The gatehouse had smoke coming from its tall chimney but although she slowed the car to a standstill, nobody came forward to take her money. Whether the season was over or Wednesday was simply a free day she didn't know, but after a few minutes she put the car back into gear and drove slowly forward between a copse of young trees on the right and a dense wood on the left. Then without warning a heavy stag deer leapt from the trees, straight across the bonnet of the car and into the copse beyond it without ever looking in her direction.

Helen slammed her foot on the brake, gripped the steering wheel and knew that her life could never be more terrifying than it was at this moment. Somehow the deer reminded her of Mark, imposing his authority on her, invading her private space with his blackmailing threats and moving away without a backward glance.

She stayed very still. The car blocked the narrow driveway so that no other vehicle could have passed her. Fortunately the girls slept on. The last thing she wanted was to

178

have to deal with them now. Her life was hard enough without adding their problems to it as well.

Eventually she moved on and had to drive right into the courtyard of the castle before she could turn round and make her way back to the main road. In all that time she didn't meet another living soul.

Chapter Thirty-Three.

Next morning Helen was exceptionally quiet as she dealt with the day to day routine of breakfast and endeavoured to shield Andrew from the worst of the chaos.

In the days before she'd had children of her own, she'd imagined him as a New Man, helping with the family, sharing the responsibility for them, but it hadn't taken long to discover her mistake. He was fiercely proud of them. He supported them financially but he was easily upset by the actual messiness of small children. One little girl might have been different, but two together defeated him. He was more at ease with Camilla than with Abi. He would put her on his knee, rest his hand against her head and prevent the jerking movements that plagued her so much. They would sit contentedly, sharing a book or quietly listening to music together, but Abi's boisterousness was alien to him. He wondered if she'd inherited it from Uncle Ernest, whose gene had given them the black hair. Perhaps he had been wild and unruly and it was only a trick of the camera that had produced such a sombre face to show to the world.

Andrew's own childhood had been ordered and secure as the only child of middle-aged parents. However, as he got older he realised that he would have exchanged it all for the rough and tumble of family life. Yet now that he had his own family he had no idea how to cope with them. It was not the automatic reaction he'd expected, so he stayed longer in the office inventing work and convincing himself that it was necessary.

When Abi and Camilla waved him goodbye Helen kissed him quickly on his newly shaved cheek and she sighed, thinking what a mess her life had become and yet she knew she could make something satisfying from it. If Mark would disappear from the scene she'd be able to relax and move freely about the grounds instead of being trapped in this blind corner of the stable yard.

Across at room 83 she could just make out the flowered pattern of the curtains pulled together behind net ones. That man - Roger something - would have to get a move on if he wanted to be on the excursion today. It would be Sedbergh, Appleby Castle and Acorn Bank Gardens, each with its special attraction. Cobbled yards, Norman keep, watermill all set in beautiful countryside that amazed the people who spent their lives in cities. But then Roger was not one of those. He came to the Lakes every Saturday if rumour was to be believed, so it seemed strange that he should choose to have a holiday here as well.

As if on cue, he drew back the curtains with a sharp flick and pulled the net to one side. Catching her staring across at him he raised his hand in acknowledgment and she automatically waved back. Then she adjusted the blind so that he couldn't intrude any further into her life.

Roger turned from the window to the small table at the side of the bed. For some unknown reason the alarm had failed to ring and it was later than he'd planned. He felt comfortable and was loath to get up and prepare for yet another coach ride. Today he would eat a leisurely breakfast and stay around the hotel or perhaps walk into Grange and treat himself to some memento of this holiday.

The dining room was emptying by the time he reached it and Andrew had already made his speech about the day's activities. It suddenly occurred to Roger that he ought to tell somebody that he wouldn't be on the coach and not let them wait indefinitely for him to appear, so after he'd ordered breakfast, he hurried along the hall to Andrew's office, gave a brief knock and went inside.

'I didn't say . . .'

'Sorry. Are you busy . . . oh,' he laughed as Andrew tried

181

to hide the local paper under a computer spreadsheet. 'It's like that is it?'

'What can I do for you?'

'I'll not be on the excursion today. I didn't want them to wait.'

'You should have told the girl. I don't deal with things like that.'

'If you've time for the paper, you've time for messages. And if you don't mind me saying you're looking a bit washed out. Is it the morning after the night before?'

'Certainly not. I'm tee-total.'

Roger shook his head, 'You should ask for a blood test then. You might be anaemic.' He left the office, closing the door loudly behind him.

Andrew winced and for the first time, he sympathised with people who really did have a hangover. Come to think of it, the man might have a valid point. He *had* been feeling down lately and if a simple course of iron tablets would fix it, it would be worth a visit to the doctor. But not just yet. He would keep an eye on the situation and hope it went away of its own accord.

We haven't seen much of Roger since Sunday night. Well, he won't be very happy about the way Mark went on at the table, but of course he's too much of a gentleman to say anything so when I see him coming out of Mr Matthews' office I dodge back under the stairs. I wouldn't like him to work out that Mark hit me and if I breathe in hard, it makes me shout. I can't help it. I've tried but it just comes out. Funny he's not on the trip today, but it'll give Mark a chance to see him later. I wish he hadn't come here. It's just made things worse.

By the time Roger had finished breakfast, half the morning had gone. The hotel had a strangely peaceful air about it and if it hadn't been for the posters and notice boards in the reception

182

area he might have imagined he was a guest in a stately home, with friends who were wealthy enough to support it. He walked quickly through it and out into the garden where a lawn mower was being driven in long straight paths that left shades of light and dark across the huge lawn.

'Roger. Over here.' It was Paul Hutchinson, his knitting needles moving rapidly in his strong hands and a new ball of wool balancing on the table in front of him.

'That wool's an exact match,' Roger indicated the closest line of grass.

Paul ignored his comment and pulled out a chair for Roger to sit on. 'Have you seen Donna since Sunday?'

'No.'

'Mark's hit her. I could bet on it.'

'Why d'you say that? Does it show?'

'No. Too clever for that, but she can't breathe without wincing. I've watched her. She tries to hide it but her breathing's shallow.'

'She might have bronchitis . . .'

'There's no cough and anyway she'd take a few days off.'

Roger nodded and thought what trouble he'd caused by coming here and how Mark hadn't deserved the help he'd given him, but he knew he'd do it all over again if it would help Donna to escape from this claustrophobic village.

'I'll try to speak to her later.'

The two men sat together, enjoying the peace of the garden until a voice from behind them broke the silence.

'You want to watch it, Roger or he'll have you knitting as well.'

Roger knew it was Mark and he had to control his temper before he turned to speak. 'Mark,' he acknowledged him with the briefest of nods.

'I'll join you,' Mark said 'and catch up on the week's news.'

'We're just going. Sorry, but we want the next train into Grange.'

Paul wound up his wool and pushed the ball on to the needles until the two points came savagely through, then he put it all into his bag and drew the zip so that nobody would have guessed it held anything more interesting than a pair of swimming trunks and a towel.

For the rest of the day, Roger kept thinking about Donna. When they passed a butcher's shop, he imagined her choosing the most economical cuts of meat to make into pies or spin out with vegetables so that the family didn't go hungry. When they sat in the park he visualised her kicking a ball for the boys or playing hide and seek amongst the trees. And then there was the picture of her with Mark . . . she would be good at that too. But if Paul was right she'd been hurt because Roger had become involved in their lives. He must find out if it was true, yet he couldn't go to the house and ask outright. He needed a reason for going. As they left the park and began to walk towards the station he said, 'What sort of things do little boys like these days?'

'Same as they ever did, I expect.'

'I liked books . . .'

'And I liked knitting, but if you're thinking of Lewis and Charlie, I wouldn't recommend that.'

'So what then?'

'Lads usually like football . . .'

'Football shirts! You're a genius. I don't know why I didn't think of it. I'm always seeing them about.'

'Which team?'

'Sunderland. You know - the Stadium of Light. Donna can take them there when she comes to her sister's.'

'They'll cost a pretty penny. .' Paul had never understood the craze for little boys to copy their football idols. Surely they didn't all crave to be footballers.

184

'It's only money and if it makes up for the trouble I've caused. . '

'Don't blame yourself, Roger. If I hadn't come to the table on Sunday, it wouldn't have happened.'

* * * * *

Roger knew he'd made the right choice when Charlie strutted round the cottage kicking at an imaginary ball and flinging his arms in the air as he pretended to save a vital goal. Lewis mimicked every action and Donna watched with pride, but Roger saw how carefully she controlled her breathing and the way she held her arms across her chest and moved her hands over her ribs. Even then she caught her breath and tried to transfer the sound into a cough.

When Roger handed her his address card she took it with a puzzled frown.

'A safe house, if ever you need one,' he said. As the boys continued their imaginary game and dribbled a ball through the living room and into the kitchen, her face turned red and she pushed her hair back showing a gold stud in her right ear.

'I don't know what you mean,' she said.

'Oh I think you do. Just keep that in a safe place.'

* * * * *

Peace of mind made Roger relax and enjoy the last day of his holiday, appreciating the beauty of the lake and the sun glistening on the water as they sailed from Bowness to Waterhead. Even the visitors' centre at Brockhole enthralled him.

When he sat with Paul in the evening watching the impromptu concert that the guests had produced, he was able to laugh at the feeble jokes and enjoy the singing, safe in the knowledge that he'd given Donna an escape route if ever she

185

needed one.

When he said goodbye to Paul next day they exchanged telephone numbers and arranged to keep in touch. However, Roger did not intend to come back to the Ascot hotel. Some things were best left alone.

I could have dropped when he gave me that card and with that writing on the back as well - "Remember I'm always here, R." I'll have to hide it. Mark would go mad if he saw that. I thought nobody'd noticed I was in pain, but he's a sharp one, that Roger. And Paul as well - he gave me a funny look the other day when I winced a bit. I wonder if they've had their heads together. It's kind of them to bother. I've never known men like that.

Chapter Thirty-Four.

Mark stood with his back to the door. Donna was good at cleaning these hotel rooms, he would say that to anybody. A freshly-laundered throw lay invitingly over the single bed. The curtains hung in perfect folds. Every surface gleamed and behind the louvered doors the old bath sparkled and the taps reflected the light from the lamp on the ceiling. He remembered how he'd come here a few months ago and stood in the very same spot, realising that Donna had obliterated Roger Keogh from the room as surely as Mark intended to obliterate him from his own life. Simply wipe him out and never think of the whole unpleasant incident again.

Now he laid the key on the bedside cupboard. The rest of the annexe was quiet at this time of day, so there was no need to lock the door. In fact it added a sense of excitement to know that he could be discovered at any time. He turned on the taps and while the water gushed into the bath he went to the window and pulled the net curtain slightly to one side.

Helen's door was closed and the slats of the blind hung only slightly apart - enough to allow a small amount of light into the room. He'd certainly made his presence felt there, he thought as he touched the wallet in his back pocket, empty now but likely to be filled before the day was out.

He was about to turn away when Andrew's car drove into the yard and stopped outside the flat. He seemed to be less jaunty than usual and Mark wondered whether it was his imagination that made him look so pale. Andrew went inside but reappeared a few minutes later with Helen close behind him then Abi rushed out and followed the car until it turned the corner and Mark watched with pleasure as she ran back to her mother, her dark hair flopping over her eyes in the same way that Lewis's did.

He returned to the bath just in time to prevent it overflowing and he grinned at the thought of spoiling Donna's handiwork. She would learn better than to make a fool of him in public. In fact it wouldn't hurt to let a little of the water splash on to the pink carpet and as for the towels, when he'd finished with them, nobody would guess they'd been put out clean that morning.

Twenty minutes later he left the room locking the door behind him and walking quickly along the empty corridor. Outside it was as quiet as he'd expected it to be in the middle of the day and he crossed the yard to the flat. He knocked and Helen opened the door just wide enough to peer out above the safety chain and would have slammed it shut but for Mark's foot placed firmly in the gap.

'Your husband's not looking well.'

'Get lost. Move that foot.'

'Watch it. I can easily put my hand round there, y'know.'

'Don't you dare . . .' From the roof top a seagull screeched its raucous cry.

'Don't dare me . . . You should tell him he needs a blood test.'

'He knows.' The gull swooped low over the yard then rose again to fly over the chimneys and away to the distant coastline.

'Does he now? And does he know it won't be the same group as the girls'?'

'It could be.'

'And pigs might fly. And that reminds me. It's pay-up time again. And don't say you haven't got it. You always give in, in the end.'

Helen gave the door a furious push, but Mark kept his foot firmly in place. 'Don't be a silly girl. I can stay here all day if need be.' He began to whistle "Twenty tiny fingers, twenty tiny toes. Two angel faces . . ."

188

* * * * *

From his first floor window Kevin stared down at the scene. He wondered whether to ring the police, but by the time they drove out here it would all be over. In fact, even now, things were happening. Mark seemed to be holding on to Mrs Matthews' arm while she spoke to somebody standing behind her. Then she reached back and brought a handbag into sight. It was black and deep and had a bright silver clasp. Only then did Mark release the grip on her arm and Kevin saw something pass from one to the other. The door was banged shut and Mark walked away smiling.

So it was still going on, Kevin thought and wondered if it would help if he went across to the flat? Or would it be better to pretend he didn't know? Perhaps the best thing might be to approach Mr Matthews and leave the responsibility to him? The one thing Kevin wouldn't do was speak to Mark. It would be more than his life was worth.

Outside, a spider's web hung crazily across the top corner of the window. The sun was just high enough to shine over the rooftops and illuminate its silken thread. Kevin watched until a small spider scuttled across the web and back again.

For the first time he wished he'd been sharing a room with the other apprentices, where he wouldn't have had a window overlooking the flat and where there would have been so much going on that he wouldn't have bothered to look out anyway. Instead the problem persisted.

But all of a sudden, the answer seemed clear. If Mrs Matthews was in trouble he must help her. She was alone with two small children and one of them disabled at that. He must go across. He had money. If she was desperate, he could offer it. A new car was not as important as this situation.

However, when he knocked at the flat there was no reply. He wasn't surprised. She was hardly likely to risk another

189

unwelcome caller. Bending down he opened the letter-box and peered inside. Red carpet and cream walls led to an open doorway and he could just make out kitchen cupboards beyond it.

'Mrs Matthews,' he called. 'Are you alright?' But there was no reply and he began to wonder if they'd gone into the yard at the back until suddenly Abi appeared in the doorway, her eyes on a level with his as they stared at each other along the narrow hall, but she was pulled quickly back by an unseen hand.

'Abi. Is your Mammy there? Tell her it's me - Kevin.'

All of a sudden, Andrew's deep voice came from behind him. 'What's going on here?' he said and Kevin was pulled roughly away from the door while Andrew felt for his keys with the other hand. 'Come on, out with it. Why are you shouting through my letter-box, like that?'

When Kevin didn't answer, Andrew shook him hard and even in his distress Kevin felt surprised at the man's strength.

'Helen. Is everything alright?' Andrew called as he pushed Kevin ahead of him into the flat.

'Daddy, Daddy. He was shouting at us and Mark came and . . .'

'Mark?' Andrew locked the door behind him, trapping them all in the confines of the flat.

'Sssh, Abi. Ssh. She makes such a drama out of everything.' Helen tried to reduce the situation to normal, but she had an anxious expression and there were tear-stains on her cheeks. 'Sorry Kevin. I couldn't come for a minute. I was doing something for Camilla.'

'But . .' Abi tried again.

'I'm sorry Mrs Matthews. I shouldn't have shouted through the letter-box.' He saw the appeal in her eyes and understood that this was something that had to be kept from her husband.

'I'm waiting for an explanation.' Andrew tapped his keys

on the nearest work-top in an irritating rhythm that obviously upset Helen.

'I was busy with Camilla when I heard the door.'

'Camilla's asleep.' Abi said her eyes large at what she was hearing.

Helen put her arm round the child in an effort to quieten her but Andrew took Abi by the hand and led her into the living-room where he switched on the television and put her favourite Cinderella tape into the video machine. Then settling her into the corner of the big settee, he left her to enjoy the unexpected treat. As she had said, Camilla was indeed asleep, but nevertheless he wheeled her chair out of the kitchen and into the living-room next to her sister.

'Now,' he said when he went back to the others. 'I'm waiting for an explanation.'

'I'll make some coffee first.' Helen said. 'Where's your car, dear?'

'Over at the hotel. Never mind coffee - - - I want to know what's going on.'

Kevin stood by the table. It was small and covered with a thick waterproof cloth. The pattern had bright cherries and green leaves and there was an egg stain at one end. Helen was making coffee from a stainless steel kettle and the beakers were yellow, with big loopy handles. Her own hand trembled slightly as she passed the first one to Andrew. 'Let's all sit down.' she said.

I don't know what's got into Mark today, but he brought a packet of sweets each for the boys and then sent them along to his Mam's so that we could have an hour to ourselves. One minute he's hitting me and the next he's making up. But I don't trust him any more and I never will.

"Come on then. I haven't got all day. You can start.' Andrew pointed a finger at Kevin.

191

'I . .er. I was going into Grange. I wondered if Mrs Matthews wanted anything bringing.'

'What - after all the time you've been here, you suddenly think she might need help?'

'Well . . with the twins and everything.'

'My wife has her own car. She doesn't need help.'

'It was just a thought.'

'You'd better have another thought then. And quick.'

'Leave it, Andrew.' Helen said.

'I won't.' he banged his hand on the table making them both jump. 'What about Wyburn?'

'Abi exaggerates.'

'But he was here?'

'Yes.'

'Why?'

'A message from Donna.'

'Why didn't she ring?'

'She couldn't get through.'

Andrew banged his hand down again. The beakers stood just where Helen had put them. Nobody had drunk the coffee.

'I want a proper explanation or *he* leaves this hotel tonight.' Andrew pointed again and Kevin knew he meant it. Mr Matthews had a reputation for saying what he meant. If only Kevin hadn't been at the window at that particular moment. In future he would look the other way when anything suspicious was going on.

He turned to Helen sitting at the end of the table. Her hair was soft as though it had just been washed and she was wearing pale blue. She had a frantic look in her eyes, half panic, half fear.

Suddenly she got to her feet, pushing the chair over behind her and slopping coffee on to the tablecloth then she lunged towards Andrew and before he realised what was happening she'd grabbed the key from where it lay beside his left hand.

192

Then she went straight towards the front door.

'You go, Kevin. Go on and thank you. Thank you for coming to help.' When he'd gone she paused then pulled herself up to her full height and ran her hands down over her hips, then she walked back into the kitchen. Andrew was standing near the sink unit, glowering in anger, but Helen spoke first. 'Are you going to throw *me* out tonight as well?'

'What's going on?'

'That's my business and what on earth d'you think you were doing, locking us in like that? It'll be all round the hotel by tonight.'

Andrew looked shocked as he realised the truth of what she was saying. 'I didn't think of that,' he said slowly.

'No . . . that's the trouble, you *don't* think and if you spent more time here you would know what was going on.' With that she walked away from him into the living room where the girls were still enthralled with Cinderella. 'Good show, is it?' she said to them.

Andrew followed and made as if to speak, but he glanced at the two little girls and thought better of it. He left the room and stormed out of the flat. Helen did not go to the window or watch him march across the yard. She was aware of his anger, but she didn't care. She had stood her ground and it felt good.

Chapter Thirty-Five.

It was nearly two o'clock before Kevin ventured into the village. He estimated that Mark must have set off by then if he had an afternoon appointment in Grange. Nevertheless when he reached the cottage he knocked and waited for Donna to let him in. Any sign of Mark and he would bolt. Or attack him but he would soon be outmatched in an open fight. Mark would overpower him in the first few minutes then walk away laughing.

As he followed Donna out into the yard and sat next to her on the old wooden bench under the window Kevin had a great urge to confide in her. Instead he simply stared out towards the distant hills.

'Penny for them,' Donna said, watching him closely.

'What? Sorry.'

'Penny for your thoughts. You've got something on your mind today.'

'It's nothing.'

'Come on, tell Aunty Donna.'

'Oh it's just Mr Matthews - he threatened to sack me last week.'

'He never did.'

'He said I'd have to go that night.' Suddenly it all poured out. How frightened Kevin had been at the thought of losing his job. How he had no other home to go to and how his savings would soon disappear if he had to pay for a room somewhere.

'You can always come here.'

'No. I can't. Not with Mark.'

'Just till you found somewhere.'

'No. He doesn't like me and I don't like him.'

Donna shook her head sadly while Kevin faced the unpalatable truth that this was only a job and he could lose it at any time. While he'd been saving and planning to move on, it had never occurred to him that he could be asked to leave. He would never feel secure again.

And now Donna was waiting for an explanation and Kevin would have to provide one. Tell her how it was nothing to do with his work and how Mr Matthews had caught him shouting through the letter-box. But she'd want to know why and what could he say? That he'd seen her own husband demanding money, not once, but twice and that he'd gone to help? No, he could never tell her that.

Kevin sat very still for a long time. Donna stayed beside him, hoping that her mere presence would be some help to him although he was so withdrawn that she wondered if he was aware of her at all. Eventually he looked at his watch and got up to go. 'It wasn't my work,' he said as if there'd been no interruption in the conversation. 'That's alright. I was trying to have a word with Mrs Matthews and he didn't like it.' With that he disappeared through the cottage and hurried away to work for several more hours.

I follow him to the door and watch him walk towards the hotel. I can't make head nor tail of what he's said but it must be something serious. Poor Kevin. I don't know what's happened. He was always the blue-eyed boy around here. It must be really bad if he won't tell me. And with this bad blood between Mark and him I can't even help him much. And it's not as if I could work out what's wrong. As far as I know nothing's happened unless Mark reminds Kevin of somebody. He's had an awful life, poor kid.

Chapter Thirty-Six.

When Andrew was asked to make an appointment to discuss the blood test he'd had the week before, he immediately thought he was dying. Cancer showed up in blood tests or rare disorders of the blood itself. And Abi's blood group had been so unusual that his must be the same. They said she'd inherited it. But it wasn't from Helen that had been proved at the time of the accident. How was it that he didn't know? Surely he should have carried a card, to warn people in case of sudden illness. What if he'd needed a blood transfusion and they'd given him some common or garden sort that didn't suit him?

Time dragged by. Four days until the appointment and four long nights when he slept fitfully and woke before dawn, giving them both a bad start to the day. However, he did not share his anxieties with Helen. He didn't want to hear reassuring words and pat phrases to calm him and make him feel foolish. Instead, he went stoically on, deluding himself that she wouldn't notice anything wrong.

On the third morning when he slid out of bed at exactly twenty-nine minutes past five and sneaked towards the bedroom door, she called after him. 'Andrew, what're you doing?'

'Sorry.'

'What's the matter?'

'Funny tummy.'

'Hotel food,' she murmured.

'Go back to sleep.'

'I can't. Once I'm awake, I'm awake.' She sat up and pulled the duvet straight. 'You must have tossed about all night,' she said, but he'd gone and she could hear the sound of water running in the bathroom. She remembered the first days of their marriage when they'd delighted in each other's company and an early start was a bonus.

Now she crossed to the kitchen and by the time Andrew came through she'd made a pot of tea and two slices of toast. But he turned to the window; a dejected figure in a towelling robe that had seen better days.

'I have an appointment,' he said, still with his back to her.

'What? . . . Where?'

'At the doctor's. Tomorrow.'

'Andrew! What's wrong?'

'It's the blood test . . . something's not right.'

A picture of Mark flashed into Helen's mind. He'd stood in the same spot the day she'd told him of her pregnancy. He'd stood tall, his head held high, as he'd rejected the idea that the child was his. Then he'd walked away. If he'd stayed life would have been so different. They'd have had to leave the hotel. She wondered where they would have settled and whether she would she have been happier. But she didn't know.

* * * * *

Andrew stared at the prescription in his hand. After all his worrying, he'd been with Dr Wainwright for less than five minutes. A cheerful man, he dealt with each patient efficiently, but wasted no time in his busy morning surgery. A straightforward case of iron deficiency he'd said. A course of tablets to put it right, see you again in a month's time. Blood type? He'd seemed surprised to be asked and Andrew had watched him check through the test results to find that it was O positive.

'No blue blood, I'm afraid,' he said. 'Just common or garden red like the rest of us. Bye Mr Matthews.'

Andrew had found himself on the other side of that solid door with a flimsy prescription in his hand and a new problem on his mind. He'd thought of rushing back in and asking for an explanation, but already another patient was coming along the

197

corridor, heading straight for Dr Wainwright's room. Andrew's chance had gone. He'd have to wait till his next appointment.

At home he said very little, trying to seem relieved that it was such a simple problem and hoping Helen wouldn't make fun of the way he'd worried. She, in turn, was happy to gloss over the incident; thankful that Andrew had made no mention of the unusual blood group.

Nevertheless, as the weeks went by, he found himself looking at Abi and Camilla in a new way, even checking the photograph of Uncle Ernest that Helen had hung so conspicuously near theirs. Of all the photographs her mother had sent her, why had she chosen to frame that one and so many weeks before her babies were born? And how was it that Abi was so boisterous when both her parents were such quiet, thoughtful people. And would Camilla have been the same if circumstances had allowed it?

Now as he lay awake at night, he managed not to disturb Helen. He wasn't ready to discuss the problem with her yet. The time for that would come later. However, one night he woke with a definite solution in his mind and wondered why it hadn't occurred to him sooner. A DNA test was the answer. A simple test for each of them. A few weeks' wait and a result that was proof beyond doubt. Easy to arrange but not always the answer you were looking for. And Andrew didn't know whether he was ready to accept the answer yet, if it turned out to be the wrong one.

Mr Matthews is looking better. Sarah says he's taking iron tablets. Mrs Matthews told her. Anyway, they must be doing him some good. He's got a bit of colour back in his cheeks and he's livelier than he's been for ages, but his temper's not up to much. I hope he doesn't take it out on Kevin again. He couldn't stay at our house now - not with the mood Mark's in

198

these days. It would be different if he had a job to go to, but he hasn't.

Chapter Thirty-Seven.

It had been a stroke of luck coming across one of the drivers like that. Not the usual place to park his lorry either, just a bit of waste ground on an awkward corner. When Mark thought how easy it would have been to miss him, he had to laugh. It was his lucky day. No mistake about it. Donna would say it was in his stars, but that was woman's stuff and he didn't believe in it but whatever it was, it couldn't have worked better.

He fingered the small packages in his jacket pocket and knew he could turn them into a healthy profit. Helen's money had come at just the right time and he'd kept it in the hope of an opportunity like this.

He stared out of the window as the train rattled its way towards home, past beaches close enough to show the ripples left behind as the tide turned and the waves retreated. But Mark was preoccupied with his own plans and the beauty of the coastline meant nothing to him.

When he left the train he nodded and smiled at people waiting to get on to it. At the post office he bought cigarettes and exchanged a few pleasantries with Mrs Monaghan and when he passed the entrance to the hotel he raised his hand to Helen as she waited to drive out on to the main road. When she deliberately turned away from him he stood quite still and watched her until she sped away into the distance. Then he patted his pocket and laughed.

When he went into his own cottage he called out to Donna and she looked up in surprise. 'You sound happy,' she said. 'Don't tell me you've found a job.'

'No. It's not worth it now. I'll have my licence back before we can turn round.'

To cover her disappointment, she said, 'that jacket's

looking dirty. Give me it here. It can go in the washer.' She put her hand on his sleeve but he shook her off.

'I've got to dash . . . .' he said and disappeared before she could pull it away from him. Upstairs, he locked himself in the bathroom, then took out the precious packets and gloated over them for a few minutes. It would be two or three days before he had the chance to sell them on and he needed a hiding place. The unpleasant experience of being arrested was one that would live with him for ever. Turning out his pockets in the police station had been innocent enough then, but would be a different thing entirely with heroin to show.

The small bathroom offered few hiding places. The high window ledge was filled with shampoos, gels and after-shave. The top of the cabinet was above eye level, but Donna was sure to dust it, as she dusted every surface in the hotel. With a flash of inspiration Mark stared at the lid of the cistern. The packets were already inside a plastic bag, so the water wouldn't seep in and damage them, and nobody was likely to look in there in the next few days. To avoid suspicion he pressed the handle and while the water flushed noisily round the toilet bowl he quietly lifted the heavy lid. To his amazement the water swirling about inside was an electric blue colour. As it settled to its normal level, he saw that Donna had put a round block of disinfectant into the tank.

'Fucking hell,' he said under his breath. What was to stop her checking on it at regular intervals? And Charlie was sure to demand an explanation of exactly why the water was blue and what was making it happen. Then Mark sighed with relief as he realised that if Donna had waited till tomorrow to put the wretched thing in, she'd have found the drugs lying there and all hell would have been let loose.

'Are you alright Mark? You've been a long time,' Donna called up the stairs, as if thinking about her had made her materialise.

'Can't a man have five minutes?'

'I'm waiting for the jacket.'

Mark pushed the drugs into his trouser pocket and threw the jacket down the stairs, on to the kitchen floor. 'I'll be down in a minute,' he called and heard her clicking the washing programme into action. He knew that if he didn't go down she'd come looking for him. The bedroom was tidy, too tidy to hide anything. Donna had hidden Christmas presents in every drawer and Mark realised that he'd never cared about privacy before. When he'd needed it, he'd used his lorry. Now his world was restricted to the cottage.

Downstairs, Donna moved back and fore across the vinyl floor. Another two steps and she'd be at the bottom of the stairs. Frantically, he stared round the bedroom, rejecting every idea as it occurred to him until in desperation, he lifted up a corner of the mattress and pushed his hand as far in as it would go. He flattened the packets against the base of the bed and was pulling his hand back, when all of a sudden, it touched something else, lying there, hidden in the blackness between mattress and base. His fingers closed round it. It was small and square and felt like cardboard.

When Mark brought it into the light he saw that it was one of Roger Keogh's address cards printed in black ink with small firm lettering. He read it slowly, bringing back memories of the terraced house and the unexpected kindness he'd found there. Then he turned the card over. On the back, in flowing handwriting, were the words "*Remember, I'm always here. R.*"

Donna was coming up the stairs, treading on the squeaky one, third from the top, then across the landing until she was there. The doorway made a perfect frame for her against the darkness of the landing.

Without a word, Mark hit her. But the impact of his fist against her face brought him to his senses and reminded him that she would be seen by all the people in the hotel. The next blow

202

was to her body.

She fell. Sprawled across the landing her head balanced over the top of the stairs. He towered above her, flourishing the small white card in his outstretched hand. 'Remember, I'm always here,' he mocked.

'Don't. It's not what you think . . .' she whispered.

'Isn't it?' he thundered. 'So why isn't this laid about eh? Why's it hidden under that mattress?'

'Because . . because . . .'

'Because I'm right aren't I? There's something going on.'

'No,' she struggled to a sitting position, reaching out to touch the wall with her left hand, keeping her right one free to protect herself against any more blows that he might inflict. He reached towards her and she flinched, but instead of hitting her he took her hand and pulled her to her feet. For a moment the walls danced round her, pale pink flowers merged with deeper pink stripes. She closed her eyes and when she opened them again, everything had settled back into its proper place.

Mark guided her roughly in to the bedroom and she slumped on the edge of the bed. 'Right,' he said. 'I'm waiting.'

She stared at him with big eyes, wanting to run. To get away. But he was there between her and the door and she knew she'd have to outwit him.

'Let's hear it, then,' he said.

'I knew you'd be like this. That's why I hid it.'

'You wasted no time, did you?' he growled. 'Did you?' He took a step forward.

'There was nothing going on . . .'

He raised his arm and she edged back towards the pillows.

'He knew you'd hit me.' It was out and instinctively she turned her head away and brought her arm up to protect herself. But the blow did not come.

'You must have told him. There was nothing to see.' Again he moved towards her.

203

'I didn't have to. He could tell.'

'Fucking thought reader is he?'

'It was the way I was breathing. I couldn't help it. You hurt me, Mark.'

Suddenly his manner changed. 'I'm sorry, Donna. I'm sorry. I love you. I'll never do it again.' He lay down beside her.

'Huh. Promises, promises,' she said, holding back the tears.

'I mean it. You're the best wife anybody could have. Honest, you are.' He put his arm round her and kissed her face where it was already beginning to turn black.

'You have a funny way of showing it,' she said, but she kept still and they lay together until noises from downstairs told them that the children had come back.

He says he's sorry and I believe him. He really is. But I don't know what's come over him. We've had our ups and downs, but he never used to hit me. It's being out of work, that's done it. And having no money.

What am I going to tell people now? I can't stay off work. They're short staffed as it is. And we're fully booked, with the Christmas House Party starting next week.

Chapter Thirty-Eight.

"Oh Come All Ye Faithful" - the carol echoed round the ground floor and floated along the landings and into the bedrooms as Mrs Kell approached the reception desk then sat at the table nearest the window waiting for her husband to re-appear. She watched new guests arriving, children gazing at the outsize baubles that hung in a fiery line across the doorway, heavy green and red streamers twisting their way up the banisters and a life-size Father Christmas pointing the way to the dining room. A magnificent Scots pine reached from the bottom of the stairs to the first floor, every branch brightened by a toy and a twinkling light and with the very same star that had been on the top since Simon was a little boy. She remembered how he'd rushed up and down and reached out in a vain attempt to touch it. She'd wanted to come this one last time to bring back those memories.

Outside, a taxi drew up to the front door and Mrs Kell recognised the familiar figure of Paul Hutchinson. He was lifting the usual old brown holdall out of the boot. She waved to him and he raised a hand in recognition. He'd come here again because Christmas at the Ascot was turning into a kind of tradition – same room, same menu, same crowd more or less. And it was preferable to being alone. He remembered Christmases at home when relatives tolerated each other for the only time in the year. They'd been good days in spite of the predictable gifts in bright wrapping papers and crackers with well-tried jokes and pathetic paper hats. The women had watched the Queen's speech while the men smoked fat cigars that filled the house with that special-occasion smell.

Later when Paul lived alone friends invited him to share Christmas with them. But eventually he'd spent it alone, walking the hills while it was daylight, returning to a frozen turkey-dinner and a pudding heated in the microwave. Afterwards he opened the bottle of whisky that was his present to himself. He didn't go so far as wrapping it in sparkly paper and deluding himself that somebody cared. He simply drank it and slept off the effects on Boxing Day.

When Mr Kell appeared with a porter carrying their cases Mrs Kell followed him up the main stairs to the best room in the hotel.

'It looks like a full house . . .' she said.

'Just one single not taken,' the porter said. 'And plenty of entertainment to keep you all busy. There's a party for the children on Christmas Eve and a treasure hunt on Boxing Day. Glad I'm not Kevin. He'll have his work cut out with all those meals . . . oh, thank you, sir,' he said and took the coins Mr Kell was holding out to him. 'Enjoy your stay.'

'I'll pop into the children's party tomorrow.' Mrs Kell said. 'It'll be an easy way of giving the presents out.'

'You bring far too much. There's no need to give to Wyburn's boys.'

'I do it for Donna. She's a nice girl and she works very hard.

'You've probably got something for her as well.'

'Just a token.'

He shook his head. 'And no doubt you've got things for Mrs Matthews and the twins.'

She laughed. 'It's going to be a lovely Christmas.'

* * * * *

At three o'clock the next afternoon she made her way to the big hall where the chairs had been moved from their formal rows and were pushed against the walls leaving space for the children to enjoy themselves. She thought of the parties she'd known where little girls wore frilly dresses and shiny shoes and played *The Grand Old Duke of York.* Today, it was disco

206

dancing and karaoke and it was hard to tell the girls from the boys with the black trousers and white tops most of them wore.

Mrs Kell was pleased to see that Mr Matthews had come and was standing near the stage with his wife and Camilla beside him. At first she couldn't spot Abi amongst the ever-increasing crowd and then she saw her, running to meet Lewis and Charlie who were just arriving with their mother. For a moment Mrs Kell was struck by the likeness between the children; not only their clothes but their stature and the way they moved and of course their very dark hair that shone in the light from the sparkling globe hanging from the middle of the ceiling. She blinked and told herself not to be so fanciful. It was nothing but her imagination. Then she went forward to speak to Donna, but stopped short at the sight of her bruised face.

'I'm a right mess, aren't I?' Donna got in first. 'And just at Christmas as well,' she smiled and tried to laugh it off.

Mrs Kell stared at her. 'Did he . . . he didn't, did he?'

'Good heavens, no. Nothing like that. I was putting the streamers up and I fell - right against the corner of the mantelpiece. Made me see stars, I can tell you.'

'As long as that's all it was.' Mrs Kell slid her presents into Donna's bag while the children were looking away, but she felt uneasy and her eyes kept going back to the ugly black mark on the side of Donna's face.

Phew. That was a near thing. Mrs Kell's lovely but she does like to know the far end of everything. I think I got it over alright though, and if she believed me, other people will. I wouldn't have come, only the boys have been living for this part and I hadn't the heart to disappoint them. The Boss's asked me to do extra hours, so the guests would have seen me then, anyway.

I might as well get it over with now. Take a deep breath. Smile. Walk across the hall.

Andrew thought how satisfying it was to watch the room fill with parents and children dressed up for the first party of the holiday all smiling and automatically moving to the rhythm of the music that floated across the room. Helen had arranged all that. Andrew knew nothing of modern music. The beginning of a house-party was always an anxious time for him, but this one had a happy atmosphere about it. He'd felt it as he mingled with the guests and spoken to them yesterday. There had been an instant response which he didn't always achieve.

Now he turned the music off and picked up the microphone to welcome not only the guests but the children of the staff who worked so hard to make the Ascot a success. It had been Andrew's idea to invite them and he'd been surprised at Helen's vehement opposition to it. She had argued heatedly, but he'd insisted, secretly afraid that without them, the hall would be only half-full. As the music began again and the older children started to dance, two small figures zigzagged amongst them, getting in the way and spoiling their fun. Andrew smiled indulgently, but secretly wondered why their mother didn't control them better. There was always one difficult family at Christmas and this was going to be it. He glanced towards Helen, intending to exchange a conspiratorial look, but she had moved forward and was making her way towards the toddlers. At the same time Donna was hurrying from the other end of the room. Andrew watched in amazement as the women grabbed one child each and hauled them to opposite sides of the dance floor. From her chair beside him, Camilla waved her arms in erratic movements and smiled her biggest smile. Andrew realised she thought it was funny and was cheering Abi on. But he wondered how he could possibly have mistaken Abi for somebody else's child.

* * * * *

On Christmas day the Kells hovered in the corridor outside the dining room until Paul Hutchinson limped into the hotel, pausing to take off his coat and hang it on the tall rack just inside the door. 'It's going to be a white Christmas,' he said, dashing a few snowflakes from his trouser legs. They walked in together and sat at the first table. Paul appreciated their kindness. He always dreaded being the odd one amongst a family party. As Kevin came to take their order, Paul eyed him carefully and was relieved to see that there were no obvious bumps or bruises like he'd had last time and he was smiling again- unlike Donna, who had appeared near the Grooms' Cottages yesterday. In the full morning light, *her* bruise had been very pronounced and her story of falling against the mantelpiece had seemed a very flimsy tale indeed.

In fact Paul didn't believe it at all. If that had been true the bruise would have been very different. It was totally impossible Paul thought. Hadn't Donna told him time and again about their ancient fireplace? That it was wooden and had a high mantelpiece that she had to reach up to but at least it was well out of the boys' way. Rage flared inside him. Donna deserved better than that and if she was prepared to take on a cripple he'd whisk them all away to his own home. He'd teach the boys to swim and paint and enjoy life. And perhaps some day they'd have other children that were his own flesh and blood. He smiled at the idea and knew he wanted it more than anything in the world. He didn't have much money but he was getting stronger every day and surely he'd earn his own living again soon. Paul knew the way Donna looked at him these days and he was sure it wasn't simply pity.

Chapter Thirty-Nine.

As the weeks went by Helen sensed a subtle change in Andrew. She caught him looking at her when she turned suddenly, only to look away again without smiling. She noticed that he spoke to Camilla first when he came into the flat and seemed out of patience with both Abi and herself. Any conversation was restricted to essentials. There was no longer day to day chat about the hotel or snippets of talk that she'd always taken for granted, but now longed to hear. There was a gap between them and she could only guess at the reason for it and hope that she was wrong. However, when she looked at her two little girls she knew that they were the most important things in her life and always would be. She smiled at them now, absorbed in their make-believe games. 'It's alright, girls,' she whispered, 'we'll have a good life together, whatever happens.'

Andrew tried to do his usual work but the children were never far from his mind. He racked his brain to recall the months before their birth. If Helen had had an affair she'd hidden it well. He'd had no reason to be suspicious, but then he'd been very pre-occupied. He'd been appointed manager of the Ascot with express instructions to turn it from a failing hotel into a very successful one and he'd done just that. Now he wondered if he'd neglected his marriage and expected too much of Helen. Looking back, he could see that she must have found life boring after living in a busy city, but he'd simply presumed that she was as committed as he was. Perhaps he'd been wrong.

Why had she been so upset when she told him that she was pregnant? And why had she flung the coffee cups to the floor and smashed them to pieces? Why had she disappeared to Brighton like that and why had she sworn him to secrecy for so long? The thoughts went round in his mind as he tried to concentrate on his day-to-day routine. His staff found him bad-tempered and moody and only approached him when it was absolutely essential, so he spent most of his days alone in the office brooding over the difficult situation. He couldn't forget the children's party and that brief moment when he'd seen Abi and Lewis as brother and sister. The likeness had been so great that there'd been no doubt at all in his mind and if this was true then Mark Wyburn must be the culprit. There could be no alternative.

Andrew thought that if it *was* true, he'd kill the man. It would be worth spending the rest of his life in jail and Helen must manage as best she could. She was no longer his responsibility . . . and neither were the girls.

The hotel's always dead at this time of the year - just the odd guest that's walking-mad. Mr Hutchinson sometimes comes, for old time's sake. He could have the best room in the hotel but he sticks with that little single in the annexe. Anyway, this is when we do the spring-cleaning and it always puts Mr Matthews in a bad temper. I think his wife must catch it, at home - she's looking really down these days. I give her a wave whenever I see her, but I never get a smile from her. Of course, it's hard having a disabled child and it's not as though Camilla's going to grow up and leave home. She's there for life and it can only get worse.

It was early spring before Paul came back to the Ascot. The days were lengthening and the light played softly across the estuary and melted the last of the snow from the hilltops. He must memorise those colours he thought and use them in his knitting. They were subtle shades that he'd not seen here before.

Mark watched Paul arrive as he took his usual Saturday morning stroll to meet Donna. Normally, the very sight of Paul would have inflamed him but now, with the renewal of his driving licence very much in his mind, he was at peace with the

211

world. He had a new spring in his step and he was easier to live with. However, he continued to demand money from Helen and rather than cause more trouble she simply handed it to him each week, but hatred for him was boiling up inside her and she was afraid that some day it might boil right over.

As Donna left the hotel she saw that Mark was sitting at one of the tables on the lawn. After the long winter it was good to see them set out again, but he shouldn't have been there and if Mr Matthews saw him there would be trouble. She hurried across to him and said, 'Mr Matthews is in the hall . . .'

'You worry too much.' His back was to the door and he didn't turn round.

'I have to work here. I don't want trouble.'

'Huh. Sitting at one of his precious tables while I wait for my wife . . what harm is there in that?'

'You know the rules . . .'

'I don't believe in rules.' Nevertheless, he stood up and with bad grace walked beside her, past the swimming pool and out towards the village. 'I'll not be meeting you for much longer, anyway.' He strode ahead.

I look at him and for a moment I wonder if he's leaving me. The idea comes as a shock and yet a small part of me wishes that he would. I'd be free then and I could to go back to the north-east and make a new life with Charlie and Lewis.

Mark's been very moody lately, out of the house for hours on end and he never says where he's been. Just carries on as usual as though I don't count. Then there's all that violence. It wasn't like him. Was it only the shortage of money and being out of work? I know that's enough to get him down but now I think was there some other reason?

'What d'you mean?' she said in a quiet voice that camouflaged her feelings. 'Where will you be?'

212

'I'll be working. Where d'you think I'll be?'

Donna breathed out - a long, slow sigh. So that was it. He'd convinced himself that some company would take him on the minute he was ready to drive. It seemed unlikely to her but she'd let him think what he liked. It was better not to contradict him.

'I've been on the phone and the boss says they're needing somebody. I knew it would work out. You worry too much. A right pessimist, that's what you are. It gets people down y'know. It's depressing, that's what it is.''

She thought of the past eighteen months and the struggle she'd had to make the money go round as well as to cope with the man himself and she wondered if he was aware of any of it.

'I'll get all the worst jobs at first, but I'll soon work my way up again.'

'That's great, Mark. Just great.' She pushed her arm through his and hoped he wouldn't realise that she was smiling at the idea of the freedom that lay ahead of her. All those hours when he would be driving his lorry and she would know exactly when he was going out and when he was coming back in, so she could relax and enjoy her two little boys again.

That evening Mark went out to celebrate, brushing aside Donna's pleas to wait until he'd got his first pay packet. A couple of drinks wouldn't do any harm and there was sure to be somebody who'd give him a lift home from the next village. The "Gun and Whistle" was unusually quiet when he pushed through the double doors and came face to face with the bar.

'Evening, Mark,' old Joe polished a glass and stood it next to a line of identical ones.

'Evening, Joe. Quiet, isn't it?'

'There's a big darts match on, in Grange. They'll be back later, either celebrating or drowning their sorrows. Either way, we'll get busy.'

'I'll just have a half.' Mark had no intention of spending the evening listening to Joe's catalogue of aches and pains.

'What're you driving these days?' Joe asked.

'Just looking out for something at the moment. I'm taking my time. I want to get the right thing.'

Joe nodded his head in agreement and Mark downed the last of his drink. 'I'll be off then. Probably look in again later when you get busy.' He crossed to the other side of the road and walked through the village, oblivious to the beauty of the flowerbeds still ablaze with daffodils and the hedges that were showing the first sign of greenery. He'd come for company and he had a nasty feeling that he was going to be disappointed.

The "Blue Bell" was set back from the road. Its ancient sign swung gently in the evening air. The white-painted door opened into a lobby with smaller doors to either side. Mark took the one into the public bar. Immediately, he knew that this wasn't his sort of place. The atmosphere was more genteel and quieter than he liked. The few people who were there sat in small groups making earnest conversation or stood in pairs at the bar. Apart from a vague nod of the head they ignored the newcomer. However, Mark ordered a pint of John Smith's and stood at the end of the bar to drink it. It didn't seem the sort of place for half pints.

Snippets of conversation reached him as voices rose and fell. The price of sheep at auction this year and the new scare that Foot and Mouth disease might have been discovered in Northumberland. If it was true it could cripple the farming community across the whole country, they said. Mark raised his eyebrows and thought it was a fuss about nothing. A few sheep - what did they matter? The farmers had it easy enough. You could tell that by the Range Rovers they drove and the quad bikes they used for covering all their acres of land. No, it was folks like Mark who had it hard. The farmers didn't know they were born. He drained his glass and walked out, as the conversations went on around him. On the forecourt, a single stone lay out of place against wooden tubs full of plants that Mark couldn't begin to recognise. He lifted his foot and with perfect aim, sent the stone hard against the wheel of the biggest Range Rover. The resounding noise it made brought two men to the door to investigate while Mark walked away, satisfied that he'd made some effect on them after all.

In his pocket the latest instalment of Helen's money waited to be spent. The notes were crisp and new this time as though she'd gone to the bank and asked specially for them instead of just taking them from her housekeeping money. He chuckled to himself as he considered whether he would stop asking for it once he was earning again. On the other hand, a little bit extra never came in wrong, did it?

He looked at his watch. It was barely an hour and a half since he'd left home, but there was nothing to keep him here. As a small blue van rounded the corner, he stepped into the road and flagged it down. Ten minutes later he was back in his own village.

I couldn't believe it when Mark was home so early. I was just settling down with a Woman's Weekly that somebody had left in the lounge. You wouldn't believe the things they throw away. Its easy come, easy go, with a lot of them, but it's alright for us. Mr Matthews knows and he says we can keep them. Anyway, I was just getting into it, when Mark arrived back with a load of drink and a temper like a demon. I knew I'd be in for it later, but what could I do? Luckily the boys were both asleep. I don't like them in amongst it.

Chapter Forty.

The impromptu supper Donna concocted so cleverly was cast aside with a disdainful glance and a few derogatory remarks, while Mark stretched himself out on the couch, a can of beer in one hand and the remote control in the other. For the time being, his temper was directed at the poor quality of the television and the fact that they didn't have a programme. He would have to spend the evening channel-hopping until he could find something to counteract the black mood he was in.

Donna managed to hide the fact that she'd missed the last few minutes of Casualty and now would never know whether the team had managed to save the pretty young woman, who'd been injured in a hit-and-run accident. She hoped they had, for the sake of the toddler in the pushchair and the nice-looking husband who'd rushed to the hospital to be with her.

'This is no good. Why didn't you get a paper?' Mark flung the remote control in the direction of the television.

'I'll pop along to your Mam's. She might have one.' It had been a choice between a newspaper and a carton of juice for Charlie's packed lunch. Donna knew which Mark would have bought.

'You know she doesn't bother with newspapers. She just switches on for Coronation Street and a few other things she likes.'

'Well, there'll be something at the hotel. It'll only take ten minutes . . .'

'Oh yes. Any excuse . . . now that Paul Hutchinson's there again. "Come and sit beside me, Paul." ' he quoted and his eyes flashed darkly. Donna recognised the signs of trouble and wondered whether she could slip past him and out of the front door. Then she remembered the boys. Asleep. Innocent and needing protection.

216

She turned towards the kitchen. She would fill the sink with hot soapy water and add a double measure of washing-up liquid until the bubbles rose to the surface and formed a complete cover for the empty bowl. Then she would pretend to wash up. She'd done it before and the warmth of the water had comforted her while the darkening window in front had acted as a mirror to let her know if Mark was following.

As the water filled the sink with maddening slowness, she put her hand in it and turned it round and round and round, while the liquid changed from solitary bubbles to a lather that grew deeper and deeper, threatening to flood the circular draining board that had always been too small for the mounds of dishes that collected after every meal.

Donna rang out a perfectly clean dishcloth and rubbed away an imaginary mark on the cold tap, then she lifted the Bizzy-Lizzy from the window-sill and wiped the flaking paintwork from left to right and back again.

Just as she was about to stand the plant back in its usual place, the reflection she'd been dreading, appeared across the glass. Grotesque, larger than life, one arm reaching out to the side. At that minute a light went on outside the house next door, and the figure was diminished. A gush of hope rushed through Donna. She knew she'd be safe as long as somebody could see her. Just as quickly, the light went out again. Either it had been switched on by mistake or they'd simply opened the door to let the cat in. Either way, Donna was alone. The fields behind, that had seemed so attractive at first, were now simply lonely places where nobody ever went.

At last she twisted to face Mark. He was closer than she'd thought. She reached out sideways for the tea-towel. Renee had given it to her and it was decorated with scenes from Disney World. Now she dried her hands on it, carefully wiping away the remaining bits of lather that clung to her left sleeve.

Mark made a grab for the towel and pulled it out of her

hand. 'I hope you're not drying my dishes with that,' he said and flicked it hard across her face.

Donna caught her breath but didn't cry out. However, she put her hand to her cheek and the gesture seemed to incense Mark more than ever.

'Don't pretend it hurt. Paul Hutchinson might believe you. I don't.'

She simply stared at him. At times like this, it was safer not to speak. Words could be misinterpreted; a wrong one could spark the violence that she dreaded so much. But now her very silence seemed to irritate him.

'Cat got your tongue, has it? Or are you just sulking?'

'I never sulk and don't you try your bully-boy stuff on me.'

The blow struck her just above the left eye. She bent her head, eyes closed, both hands covering the injury. When she had convinced herself that there wasn't any blood she slowly lifted her head and looked. To her amazement the room was empty. The house was quiet. Apart from the tea-towel lying like a rag in the middle of the floor, there was no evidence of the row at all.

Slowly, she climbed the stairs. Charlie and Lewis were sleeping, black hair spread across brightly patterned pillowslips, contented murmurs escaping from baby lips. She stood for a moment looking down at them. Tomorrow they would leave together. Whether Mark was back or not, they would go. One way or another she would trick him and they would escape. There would be no coming back.

I go to the other bedroom and lie down on my side of the bed. I don't turn the covers back and I don't get undressed. I just lie on top, resting my body till its light again. I'll need plenty of energy tomorrow. You never know what I'll have to cope with then.

Chapter Forty-One.

Mark walked with determined steps. Both hands were clenched into fists as he swung them back and fore with military precision. He'd had to get away from the cottage or he wouldn't have been responsible for his actions.

Now he headed straight for the hotel but ignored the main entrance and walked on until he reached the wicket gate and the twisting footpath through the trees. His steps were muffled by the damp grass and his shadow was just one more to add to those of the tall trunks and bare branches of the overhanging trees.

A few lights still shone from the ground floor lounges but as he got closer, it was obvious that the Reception desk was closed for the night. He fingered the key in his pocket. It seemed unlikely that room 83 would be occupied but he would need to take care. Turning sharply to the right, he headed for the Grooms' Cottages and the Stable Yard. As he reached one of the ornate lamp standards set alongside the footpath a figure approached from the opposite direction. Mark put his head down and would have simply nodded as he passed.

'Evening, Mr Wyburn.' It was Kevin, hurrying back to the hotel on a last- minute errand.

Mark grunted a reply and walked on. Ignoring the steps to the annexe he went straight round to the Stable Yard. A light shone from Helen's living-room, as it would do until Andrew was home for the night he supposed. Or maybe he was there already, sharing a bed-time drink and playing at happy families with Helen. Mark walked just far enough into the yard to see that room 83 was in darkness. He was almost sure that the curtains were still drawn back.

Swiftly he retraced his footsteps, tried the outside door and sighed with satisfaction when it opened to his touch. The corridor was silent. Without checking the windows from outside there was no means of knowing whether the other rooms were occupied. At the end of the corridor he slid his key quietly into the lock and slowly turned it. Already an apology was on his lips in case the bed was occupied and he startled a guest into hysterical screaming. However, as he'd thought room 83 was empty. He put the key back in his pocket, closed the door and went into the ensuite bathroom. Without a window it was safe to switch on the light otherwise he'd have had to wait until the Matthews' flat was in darkness and there was no chance of them seeing him.

It seemed only a few minutes until their light went out but Mark spent the time imagining Andrew and Helen settling down for the night in the room that had once been so familiar to him. He wondered whether it had changed since those days - new curtains, different wallpaper. But the greatest change of all was in the second bedroom, where Abi and Camilla were sleeping now. And that fool of a man didn't suspect anything.

As soon as he was in bed a satisfying sleepiness came over him and he stretched out his hand and pulled the curtains together.

* * * * *

In the next room, Paul Hutchinson lay reading a crime novel that Mr Kell had recommended but it wasn't holding his attention. In fact, the whole week was turning into a disappointment. Since the holiday he'd shared with Roger he'd begun to realise what a lonely existence he usually had. This was probably the last time he would come to the Ascot. Even the Pool had lost its attraction now that he'd mastered the technique of swimming again. As the hours passed he thought of the people that he might miss. Mr and Mrs Kell - but then they wouldn't be coming for much longer. Mr Matthews who'd always been courteous and made sure Paul had the room he liked, and Kevin who knew Paul's taste in food and served it without fuss.

Then there was Donna, and if he was honest Donna was the main reason for his decision. Everything about her was good. Her pretty face, her gentle nature, her kindness. She deserved the best in life and he would like to give it to her but he wasn't one to break up a marriage, not yet anyway, but he was watching and he was planning and when the time was right he'd make a move.

He flung back the duvet and angrily grabbed the artificial leg that stood close by. He hated the thing, resented the limitations it put on him but when it was strapped into place he felt more of a man and moved about the room with confidence. Three o'clock in the morning was a bad time to be awake especially when the rest of the hotel was so silent. He hadn't seen anybody else in this annexe since he'd arrived, so he presumed he was the only one there. In fact he might be the only person in the whole world at this moment. Suddenly, he needed to reassure himself that there *were* other people out there somewhere, so he switched on his radio. Music filled the room. He recognised the voice of David Bowie. How could he ever forget the eighties? He'd been a young man then with his whole life ahead of him.

> *"Let's dance*
> *Put on your red shoes and dance the blues.*
> *Let's dance*
> *to the song they're playing on the radio."*

And he *had* danced with the rest of them. Paul shook his head sadly now but he began to hum to the music and slowly he relaxed until he was able to sit in the armchair and wait for the kettle to boil.

Without warning the pipes in the wall began to rattle and to bang. He could hear water splashing into the bath next door.

To crown it all a discordant voice sang, *"Oh what a beautiful morning. Oh, what a beautiful day."*

Paul got to his feet. Mark Wyburn! Using that room again. He had no right to be there and what about Donna? Why wasn't he at home with her? Paul was half inclined to walk across to the village now, early as it was and knock at her door and tell her exactly what that husband of hers was doing. For a few minutes he toyed with the idea imagining Donna opening the door as she pulled a pretty dressing gown over a flimsy nightie in her haste to let the boys sleep on.

He paced around the room tossing the idea about in his head, picturing her walking back with him into this building and along the corridor to number 83 but then doubt crept in. How would Mark react? He would be angry certainly. He might even hit Donna. He certainly wouldn't walk quietly back through the garden and out to the village like a naughty schoolboy. In any case Donna wouldn't leave the children alone in the house Paul was sure of that. But it wasn't fair on Donna and Paul intended to put an end to it once and for all.

He hurried to the door then stopped dead in his tracks. It would have to be done carefully. A foolish rush was just what Wyburn would be expecting and Paul would easily be beaten. He took time to pull a dark green track suit over his pyjamas then he looked round for something to use as a weapon. His knitting needles lay by the bed with bright red wool ready to be cast on. He picked them up and practised lunging forward and jabbing them into his pillow. But they weren't strong enough and he rejected the idea as useless.

Next door, the splashing reached a new crescendo. Mark must be topping up the level of the water and the tap was running again. Paul scoured his bedroom for something to use. His spare leg was there but it was too light. If he used his walking stick Mark might wrench it out of his hands and mock him as he did so.

Then his eye fixed on the reading lamp. It was made from some sort of ornamental stone and it was brutal. However Paul felt sure he could lift the lamp with one hand and balance himself with the other so he picked it up and experimented with its weight. He wouldn't be able to carry it for long but his door was very close to the next one so it would only be a matter of minutes.

First he removed the shade then he pulled the plug out of the socket and wound the flex round his wrist. He grasped the lamp by its narrower top and upended it. As the music from the eighties clashed with Mark's songs from the shows Paul unlocked his door and balanced his way along the corridor until he could press the handle of room 83. As he'd thought it was unlocked.

The room was lit by an identical lamp to his own. Extra light was streaming out from the alcove where both the pine doors were opened wide. Mark sat in the bath, his back to Paul while steam rose round him, bleaching the blackness of his hair and lightening the clothes laid on the shelf behind him. At that moment Paul hated Mark more than he'd ever done before - his arrogance, his cruelty, his total self-confidence.

Paul's feet sank into thick carpet. He moved forward and brought the heavy lamp down on to the back of Mark's head in a single blow that silenced him for ever.

Something wakes me up. I go down and make myself a drink. He might be lying on the couch. I didn't hear him come back, but I don't know where else he could be at half past three in the morning.

224

Chapter Forty-Two.

As soon as it was light Donna began to plan for the day ahead. She would take as much as they could carry, but there would be a lot to leave behind so she had to think carefully. The very need to think about the future blotted out the present and she was able to move swiftly through the house, pushing clothes into bags, testing their weight as she went along. Charlie might carry one small bag, but Lewis would do well simply to walk along beside them.

As soon as she could find out the times of trains, they would be off and they would never come back. She stood still for a minute and took stock of the house that had been home for so long. There'd been good times as well as bad. Mark had been a rough diamond, but she'd loved him . . . and still did in a crazy way. She hesitated and wondered whether to give the marriage one last try, then she remembered last night's scene and pushed her newest shoes into the hold-all. Best to wear comfortable ones for the journey, it could be a long day. It was lucky that yesterday had been pay day, she'd need every penny she could get now.

Thinking of that, she opened the under-stairs cupboard and rummaged at the back for her tabard. She always hid her wages on Saturdays when Mark went out for a drink. Now she lifted coats off pegs and moved boots from back to front, tipping them upside down and shaking them vigorously. A cold chill went through her and she thought back to the previous day when Mark had been sitting at the table on the lawn and she'd hurried out to move him. She'd never gone back in. The tabard would be lying where she'd left it . . . and the money would be in the pocket. She would have to get it, but Sunday was her day off and she'd been thankful that nobody would see her latest bruises.

But if she ran she might be there and back before the boys woke or anybody else was about.

As a precaution she took the path through the garden, as Mark had done the night before, then she let herself in to the hotel. The tabard was there, exactly where she'd left it, the wage packet intact. With a sigh of relief, she put the money in her jacket pocket, then stared round as though she was seeing the hotel for the first time. Suddenly she wanted a last look. She peeped into the main rooms and daringly went up the stairs and along the landings, until she came to the part that led to the Grooms Cottages and was used by the staff only. The carpet was shabby and there was a cobweb hanging from the light. She would deal with that tomorrow . . . then she remembered - there wouldn't be a tomorrow.

As she passed Kevin's door she had a mad hope that he might come out and she could tell him where she was going, but he didn't. Downstairs, there was an eerie silence. Paul would be in room 82, but it was better that he didn't know what was happening. He'd been looking at her in a different way lately and she didn't want Mark to blame him after she'd gone.

Room 83 was usually empty. Now the door was open. Automatically, Donna moved forward to shut it. A tiny scrap of red wool had stuck to the wood just near the handle, but she didn't see it. Unable to resist a final peep, she stepped into the room. The lights were on. She moved forward, then stifled a scream as she saw the body in the bath full of water. The head was bent forward so that the face was hidden. On the back of the skull there was a gaping wound. Blood had congealed around it and run down on to the man's neck and shoulders, turning the water to a murky shade of red. His right hand still held on to the silver handle at the side of the bath while his body slumped the opposite way.

In spite of the terrible injury Donna knew at once that it was Mark. With a frantic need to see his face, she snatched one

226

of the towels that she'd left there herself, yesterday morning, then she forced the head up and the whole body back until it rested against the end of the bath. The water was so deep that the body slipped down and the face went under. Mark wouldn't have minded, she thought desperately. He'd always liked to swim underwater.

I feel nothing. All these years. I feel nothing.
Mark's dead. He's not coming back. They know about the rows we've been having.
I'll be arrested. They'll lock me up.
I've got to get out of here.
Thank god the cleaners don't do the rooms on Sundays. I'll have twenty-four hours. The train. . . . I'll get the train.

Chapter Forty Three.

Charlie's been crying all the morning and now he's keeping close to me but he's got tight hold of the carrier bag with his Sunderland strip in it.

A train comes screeching through the station and everybody jumps back. 'Go and sit over there,' I tell him and point to where our Lewis sits on the old bench with the dark leather cover. He's being really good. His bag's on the floor. He's not that keen on football yet.

I pull myself together and go to the ticket office, but I have to speak up to make them hear through the glass.

'How do I get to Durham?' If Renee had been at home I'd have gone to Sunderland, but it'll have to be Durham now and the rest of the way in the bus.

'What . . .now?' The man behind the window looks surprised as though he's never sold a ticket for Durham before. Anyway he checks his computer and looks at the clock on the wall above his head, then he says '12.15. Platform 2. Change at Carlisle and Newcastle.'

No easy ride this is going to be and we've already changed once. I fish my old black purse out of my bag. I've been promising myself a new one for years but there's never enough left over.

'Me and the two boys,' I say. He looks across at them. 'They're seven and four,' I say.

'Pity,' he says. 'If the little one had been a bit younger I needn't have charged.'

I kick myself. Every penny counts now.

'Returns is it?'

I look through the glass in the top half of the white door and out to the car park. Beyond it traffic rushes past on its way back to Hill Edge.

'Singles,' I say and pull two folded notes from the old purse.

'Lewis. Charlie. Bring your bags.' I set off towards the platform. The paintwork's all done red and hanging baskets splash a bit of colour about but the hills are empty today and you can see the smoke from the fires that are burning the animals from that terrible Foot and Mouth disease. I'll not be sorry to get away.

Some people are still wearing hiking boots even though most of the paths are closed. They have their haversacks by their feet ready to jump on to the train that'll take them back to Birmingham or Oxford or Brighton. I push my way through, I know the boys'll follow me. They've lost one parent, they won't want to lose another but still I glance over my shoulder before I go down the steps to the tunnel that takes us under the line and up to the platform where the trains go to Carlisle and then on to Glasgow.

Our footsteps sound hollow and Charlie can't resist whispering 'Hallo .o. o.' Lewis giggles and I remember it was Mark who taught them to make the echo. There's a roar above our heads. 'Quick, the train's here. They only stop for two minutes.' The three of us run as if our lives depend on it.

When the train leaves Penrith station I'm too busy balancing my way along the carriage between sticking-out feet and awkward luggage, to take stock of what's happening. By the time we've squeezed ourselves into a seat meant for two we're hurtling away from the old life and the hills are turning into level ground.

I wonder what sort of reception Mam'll give us. She mightn't be too pleased especially when she realises we're not going back.

229

By 9 o'clock a hazy sun was trying to break through the mist that hung over the Ascot Hotel and Paul was already established in the garden at the table with the clearest view of the annexe. But he wasn't knitting. He was simply breathing in the fresh air and savouring the beauty of his surroundings. His work had always been to save lives, now he'd destroyed one, but he didn't regret what he'd done. Mark deserved to die.

The morning passed and half the afternoon while guests came and went, carrying coffee in white cups or cold drinks in tall glasses. They smiled as they passed and Paul acknowledged them with a brief nod of the head. Still nobody found Mark's body until at last Paul watched a new guest walk from the main door of the hotel to the Grooms' Cottages.

Then the furore broke. The peace of the hotel was shattered by screeching sirens, blue lights and scene-of-crime officers. And still Paul sat. Nothing would link *him* to the murder. He replayed the scene in his mind over and over again; the way he'd used the lamp from his own room and replaced it meticulously afterwards. He even remembered to wipe the door handle with the cuff of his sleeve.

In the distance the afternoon train hooted as it left the Halt and lorries rumbled through the village on their way to the motorway. Just then Helen Matthews appeared with her two little girls beside her. They crossed the grass towards Paul and it occurred to him that she looked calmer than he'd seen her for a long time. She sat down beside him and without preamble she said, 'Mark's dead. Have you heard?' But before he could answer she went on, 'And Donna's gone.'

'Donna?' Paul stared past the swimming pool and out towards the village that had been Donna's home for so long. His face was ashen, his eyes wide.

'Yes, they say she must have left first thing this morning. She's taken Lewis and Charlie with her of course.' Helen

230

gathered her own children closer to her. 'I'm not surprised she's snapped. But I never thought she'd kill him. . . .'

'Donna didn't do that.' The words exploded from Paul's mouth and despair contorted his face into a hideous mask. He pulled himself to his feet. 'It wasn't Donna. It was me. I killed Mark.' Without another word he left them and limped away across the lawn towards the Grooms' Cottages where policemen swarmed around the entrance.

Helen couldn't move. She stared unbelieving until Abi tugged at her hand. 'Mr Hutchinson's left his bag, Mummy. It's got all his knitting in it – he'll need that won't he?'

Helen picked up the bag and they crossed the lawn, Camilla's wheelchair bumping on the rough grass but before they could catch up with Paul they saw him being guided into a police car, an officer's hand firmly on the top of his head. Then the door was slammed. The little group watched as the car turned on to the main drive. They waved and held up the bag of knitting but Paul gazed stonily ahead as the car gathered speed and disappeared into the village.

Helen hurried away wheeling Camilla home to the flat although the child waved her arms out making it very clear that she wanted to stay near Abi. Helen felt cold inside and in spite of the sunshine that broke from behind the clouds she thought she'd never be warm again.

Mark was dead.

She could hardly believe that she was free from him at last yet she remembered how she'd welcomed him in those early days when Andrew had been too busy to notice her and life had been so desperately lonely. But she'd never meant it to become serious, not even when the girls were born. If Mark had kept away from them it could all have worked smoothly.

As she opened her own front door she thought of the day she'd seen Donna doing that same thing and how incensed it had made her feel. Now Donna had gone and taken her little boys

231

with her. Helen hoped she would make a new life for herself. None of this had been her fault. She stepped into the narrow hallway where empty cardboard boxes were piled one on top of the other. Suddenly there were footsteps in the yard outside and Abi shot past Helen and out of the front door. 'It's Daddy,' she called.

Andrew had come from the hotel and was walking towards them with a lighter step than he'd had for a long time, much as he'd done when Helen first met him. Abi grabbed his hand and they came into the flat together. Helen walked into the kitchen but he followed her.

'What are all these boxes doing here?' he asked.

Helen drew herself up to her full height and turned to face him. 'I'm moving out,' she said.

Abi looked from one to another and Andrew put his arm round her shoulders and guided her from the kitchen. Then he turned back to Helen and said, 'But you've nowhere to go.'

'I'm going home to Brighton. There's plenty of room for us all and the family have promised to help with the girls.'

Andrew sat down hard on a kitchen stool. 'I didn't think you'd really do it,' he said. 'And what about the career you wanted so much?'

'It's all arranged. I'm going back to my old store . . . '

'So you've done all this without telling me? . . . . .?'

Helen shrugged her shoulders. 'You haven't wanted to know.' She stared at him. His hair seemed to have a bit more life in it these days and one strand had fallen over his brow so that she wanted to go and straighten it for him.

'I had my priorities wrong, I see that now,' Andrew said.

She let him go on.

'But this is a terrible business with Wyburn and to think that poor chap Paul Hutchinson will be locked up for years! It really puts things into perspective doesn't it?'

Helen didn't reply.

232

'When we first came here I thought we'd have a perfect life together but I should have known how much you'd miss the town-centre store and all your friends. I've been very selfish Helen, I didn't realise.' He looked as though he might weep and Helen took a step towards him but he put out a hand to stop her and then he went on, 'Is it too late to start again? You're the only girl I ever wanted . . . '

'What about the children? You *do* know don't you . . . '

He nodded and stared out of the window. 'I realised at Christmas and I thought I could live without you all, but I can't. We've been a family ever since they were born and we could go on being one. We can buy a house in the village and we can afford help now. Will you try again Helen? Please.'

She turned away and stood with her back to him for a few minutes – Andrew was standing on the exact spot where the French beakers had been broken all that time ago. She thought how Mark had stormed out of the kitchen that afternoon and how she'd needed to take out her anger on something. Now she looked at Andrew. 'Abi and Camilla have taken after Mark, not me . . . '

Andrew laughed. 'I thought they were a throw-back to great Uncle Ernest.' Helen blushed and he went on. 'So we can get rid of that awful photograph at last.'

She nodded then said, 'Abi has a temper you know.'

'Abi's wonderful, just as she is.'

'But what about Camilla? She'll never be any different, it's going to be a lifetime's commitment.'

Andrew stepped towards her. 'I'm ready for all of it,' he said. He lifted two beakers from their hooks below the wall-cupboard. They were decorated with pictures of Lakeland sheep.

'We'll have a quick cup of coffee then we'll just catch the estate agents in town.'

While the kettle boiled Helen stood at the small window

that overlooked the yard and she thought of the life they would build together. The children would grow up in a spacious house with a dream kitchen and views of the bustling village and the peaceful estuary beyond.

Lightning Source UK Ltd.
Milton Keynes UK
04 March 2011
168660UK00001B/20/P